DEATH AND THE DECORATOR

DEATH AND THE DECORATOR

Simon Brett

SEVERN
HOUSE

First world edition published in Great Britain and the USA in 2022
by Severn House, an imprint of Canongate Books Ltd,
14 High Street, Edinburgh EH1 1TE.

Trade paperback edition first published in Great Britain and the USA in 2022
by Severn House, an imprint of Canongate Books Ltd.

severnhouse.com

British Library Cataloguing-in-Publication Data
A CIP catalogue record for this title is available from the British Library.

ISBN-13: 978-0-7278-5067-6 (cased)
ISBN-13: 978-1-4483-0929-0 (trade paper)
ISBN-13: 978-1-4483-0923-8 (e-book)

All Severn House titles are printed on acid-free paper.

MIX
Paper from
responsible sources
FSC
www.fsc.org   FSC® C013056

Typeset by Palimpsest Book Production Ltd.,
Falkirk, Stirlingshire, Scotland.
Printed and bound in Great Britain by
TJ Books, Padstow, Cornwall.

To Donald,
who must have painted
every square centimetre of Frith House,
inside and out

ONE

'Oh, for heaven's sake!' said Carole Seddon testily. 'You're not going to tell me that colours have emotions?'

'I didn't say that,' came the even reply from Jude. 'Colours do not *have* emotions. They *prompt* emotions.'

'Huh,' said Carole.

It was a response Jude had heard many times before. And entirely predictable. Jude privately berated herself for the ease with which she kept putting herself into contention with her neighbour. Carole Seddon could be very prickly and there were whole acres of subject matter which were best avoided. The trouble was, though, that if Jude never ventured into areas that might spark scepticism from Carole, they'd never have anything to talk about. And they were, in their own idiosyncratic way, very close.

The topic which had engendered the 'Oh, for heaven's sake!' and the 'Huh' in this instance was decoration. Jude, seated over coffee in the antiseptic magnolia-walled kitchen of her neighbour's house, High Tor, had casually mentioned that she was about to have her sitting room painted.

There were few subjects she could raise that didn't prompt suspicion in her neighbour. Jude had long since ceased to mention anything about her emotional or romantic life. The fact that she had two marriages and a number of affairs behind her had, from their first meeting, engendered competitive jealousy in Carole. Her own arid marriage to – and subsequent divorce from – David had left her feeling bruised and unlovely. And her one foray into relationships since had been unlikely and, in retrospect, ill-advised.

So, the arrival next door, some years before, of a woman who seemed at ease with herself and wielded a measurable magnetism for men, had set Carole's self-disparagement machine into instant overdrive. She felt convinced that Jude's tally of lovers far exceeded the number that she could possibly have crammed into her fifty-odd years of life.

As a result, whenever possible, Jude kept off the subject of men.

She also tried to keep off the subject of her working life. She was a healer. And the word had only to be spoken to prompt gales of scepticism from the direction of High Tor. It was Carole Seddon's view that anything that couldn't be treated on the NHS didn't deserve treating. That alternative and complementary therapies were 'mumbo-jumbo'. And that mental illness was all in the mind.

'So, colours can heal, can they?' asked Carole.

'I didn't say that.'

'Some people's cancers can be healed by a dab of emulsion? Is that it?'

'You know full well it isn't. But the right choice of colours can contribute to a healing environment.'

Carole restrained herself from giving vent to another 'Huh.' Instead, she asked, 'Why suddenly now?'

'I beg your pardon?'

'Why do you suddenly want to redecorate Woodside Cottage now?'

'Why not now?'

'I don't know. But since you moved to Fethering, Jude, you've seemed quite happy living in a state of . . .' She hesitated. Jude wondered whether her neighbour was on the brink of 'chaos' or 'squalor', before Carole continued, more graciously, 'to have the house the way you like it.'

'Oh, I've just been thinking it needed doing for a while.'

'I see.' It was a tacit acknowledgement that she wasn't going to get any more information, but Jude knew the real, unspoken question was about money. Carole was eternally intrigued about what her friend lived on. Surely it wasn't from healing – there couldn't be a living in that, could there? Where did Jude's income derive from? Was it, Carole's suspicious mind speculated, payments from still-besotted former lovers?

Jude had no intention of revealing that what had enabled the employment of a decorator was an unexpected legacy from one of her former clients. An old woman, whom she had treated over the years for panic attacks, had bequeathed a grateful couple of thousand to 'Jude, my healer and friend, with love.'

Carole returned to the scab she'd been scratching earlier. 'So, what is this about colours prompting emotions?'

'There is a view,' Jude replied, 'that certain colours encourage certain moods.'

'Whose view?' came the sharp response.

'How far do you want me to go back?' asked Jude wearily. 'According to some authorities, chromotherapy originated with the Egyptian god Thoth.'

'"Authorities"?' Carole echoed cynically. 'By that I suppose you mean New Age birdbrains?'

Jude hadn't the energy to get into another of these circuitous arguments.

But, needless to say, Carole wasn't finished. She selected another word to repeat with the same dismissive intonation. '"Chromotherapy"? Giving something a medical-sounding name doesn't stop it from being mumbo-jumbo, you know.'

Jude looked at her watch. It had a large round face and was threaded onto a colourful ribbon tied around her wrist. 'I have to go,' she said abruptly. 'Someone coming to see me.'

'Patient?' asked Carole.

'As you know, I prefer to use the word "client",' said Jude, for the umpteenth time.

'So, is it a *client* or . . .?'

Jude was amused by the absent words. '. . . or another of your lovers?' But, however much she thought that, Carole would never say it.

'Someone I'm mentoring,' Jude said as she rose from the table.

'"Mentoring"? Nobody had *mentors* when I was growing up.'

'I think people did, Carole, but they probably called them something else. "Teachers"? "Tutors"? "Apprentice-masters", possibly?'

That got another 'Huh'. Then, 'By the way, who're you getting to do your decorating?'

'Pete. Have you heard of him?'

'Oh yes. Everyone in Fethering knows Pete.'

Jude waited for the critical remark that followed the mention of most local names.

But it didn't come. Instead, Carole said, 'Apparently, he's very efficient, Pete. Nobody has a bad word to say about Pete.'

'Good.' By now, Jude was at High Tor's front door. When she opened it, she felt the icy blast of February in Fethering.

'When it comes to colours for walls,' Carole called after her, 'you can do a lot worse than magnolia.'

There is nothing so beguiling as enthusiasm, particularly in the young. Jude had felt that the moment she met Brandie Neville. It was at a Complementary Health Conference in Bristol. Jude had been on a panel discussing the subject: 'How to Convince Sceptics that Healing Works'. She had taken on the assignment with some reluctance. She didn't really like talking about her work. Though she never doubted its efficacy, discussing healing in public seemed somehow threatening, a risk to its fragile mystery. But the organizer of the event, a therapist friend called Chrissie, had convinced her that unpersuaded members of the audience might be won round by her good sense and straight talking. (And Jude's argument that there were unlikely to be many 'unpersuaded members of the audience' attending a Complementary Health Conference was given very short shrift.)

It was after the end of the discussion that Brandie Neville introduced herself. She was small and dainty, there was something almost fairylike about her. Her voice was small and dainty, nearly childish, too.

And very tentative. Nervous, even. It was clearly costing her something to approach a stranger.

'I so enjoyed what you said in the discussion, Jude. It is all right to call you "Jude", is it?'

'That's what everyone else calls me,' was said with an easy smile. Jude's maiden name and the surnames of her two husbands were rarely spoken.

'What really interested me was what you said about . . . the gift of healing.'

'Oh, yes?' There was a small note of unease in Jude's voice. Experience had taught her that this remark could provide the opening for a torrent of scepticism.

But she had misjudged Brandie. 'It must be wonderful to have that gift. When did you first realize that you'd got it?'

'Hard to say. I had various other careers and found that friends and colleagues used to come to me with their troubles. Usually emotional troubles, it turned out, but whereas some people might have regarded that as an imposition, I was surprised to find I welcomed it. And, though usually I started with just talking to help my . . . "clients", I suppose even then was how I thought of them . . . I found increasingly I was incorporating massage. I've always known instinctively the links between the mental and the physical. Holistic seems the only sensible approach. So, I suppose you could say that, rather than me finding healing, healing found me.'

'Have you got time for a coffee?' asked Brandie.

Jude acceded to the request, though she normally welcomed a bit of time on her own after taking part in a public event. No one would have detected it from her unruffled exterior – and one of her many former careers had been as an actress – but she still found being in front of an audience took it out of her. Like many people who met the public with apparent ease, at Jude's core was an introvert. She regularly needed the restorative powers of solitude.

Complementary Health Conferences don't command major venues. The Bristol one took place in a former Edwardian primary school which had been repurposed as an arts centre. It had a bar and, by then being late afternoon, Jude decided she'd have a glass of New Zealand Sauvignon Blanc. She had to hang around till the end of the day's proceedings, anyway. There was a dinner scheduled with the organizer Chrissie and her wife Karen. So, she might as well start drinking now.

Brandie said she'd have a Sauvignon Blanc too and offered to pay for them. But Jude insisted they each bought their own. She didn't want to be beholden to someone she didn't know. Besides, Brandie looked young enough to be an impoverished student who could ill afford standing drinks for people.

When they were settled with their wine, the girl asked for more detail about her new friend's route into healing. As she spelled out the journey, Jude surprised herself by the randomness, but also inevitability, with which she had found her vocation. It had been her destiny for a long time. As she had the thought, she was conscious of how Carole would have pooh-poohed any talk of destiny, particularly in connection with healing.

She also told Brandie about the people who had acted as her

mentors, and how knowledge gained at Complementary Health Conferences, like the one they were attending, had helped develop her skills. Minds should always be open to new ideas.

'Mostly,' she concluded, 'healing's one of those things you learn by doing it. With each client you become more proficient. You increase your store of knowledge. Though all of them are different, all are individuals, certain themes recur. Certain conditions recur, and you get better at knowing how to treat them. It's a continual learning process.'

'But not everyone could learn it, could they, Jude?'

'I think very few people could be bothered to. Most would find many other sorts of job considerably more appealing. And considerably more lucrative, come to that.'

'But it's more than a job, isn't it?'

'What do you mean?'

'It's a gift, isn't it?'

'I suppose it is,' said Jude cautiously.

'No amount of learning could make you able to do it if you didn't start off with the gift.'

'Probably not.' A moment to reconsider. 'No, certainly not.'

'Well, what I want you to tell me, Jude,' said Brandie intensely, 'is whether I've got that gift . . .?'

The question had still not been fully answered to Jude's satisfaction. But there was no denying Brandie's enthusiasm.

It turned out that she wasn't a student. Perhaps her diminutive stature made her look younger, but she was nearer thirty than twenty. And a bit vague about her background. Jude didn't mind that. When it came to discussing her past, she wasn't a completist either. She always tried to answer questions honestly, following the time-honoured Jesuit principle of telling the truth, but not necessarily the whole truth.

It was serendipitous that Brandie did not live far from Fethering. She was currently renting a flat in a converted stable block on the edge of the South Downs, just north of Fedborough in the valley of the Fether.

And she was genuinely interested in the business of healing, one of those people who, on acquiring a new preoccupation, wanted to find out as much about it as possible. Already, Brandie's range of reading on the subject far exceeded Jude's own. And she had recently become obsessed by the literature of *chakras*.

But that Wednesday afternoon, as she left the kitchen of High Tor, there was no way Jude would have told Carole either of two facts. First, that the person she was mentoring was called Brandie. Or, second, that she and Brandie were going to discuss the new decoration of Woodside Cottage, based on the colours associated with different *chakras*.

'The main issue of the Third Eye *chakra*,' said Brandie, 'is intuition and wisdom. It kind of represents the Sixth Sense. And the colour associated with it is indigo.' She looked round the cluttered sitting room. 'I could see this in indigo, you know.'

Jude screwed up her face. 'I've never really liked indigo as a colour . . . and I'm not so pretentious as to believe I'm offering intuition and wisdom.'

'I'm sure that's what your clients think they're getting from you.'

'I wouldn't know. As I've said before, Brandie, a lot of what I do is just intuitive. I don't like analysing it too deeply.'

'But you must think about it,' Brandie insisted. 'What do your clients get from their sessions with you?'

'I suppose what I want them to get is . . . well, to feel better.'

'Emotional balance?'

'If you like.'

'Because that,' said Brandie with something like triumph, 'is the main issue of the Sacral *chakra*! And the colour associated with the Sacral *chakra* is orange.'

The prospect of a sitting room painted orange did not appeal to Jude. 'I think really what I want to give to my clients is a sense of empowerment. Yes, I may have helped them, but the healing has to come from within themselves. I want them to leave a session feeling confident that, with my guidance, they will in time be able to manage their own problems. That I've, in a way, enabled them to stand on their own two feet.'

'Ah, *manipura*!' said Brandie. 'The third *chakra*. The Solar Plexus. Its main issues are Personal Power and Self-Will. That's what you're talking about really, isn't it?'

'I suppose so.'

'And its colour is yellow!'

'Hm.' Jude smiled and looked at her large round watch. 'Well, you've given me lots to think about, Brandie.'

'Oh, I'm sorry. Have I been wasting your time?'

The reaction was so immediate, the girl's vulnerability so near the surface, Jude found herself instantly in reassurance mode. 'No, no, it's fine. I'm just due somewhere else shortly.'

'You don't mind me coming round, do you?'

'No, of course I don't.'

''Cause do say if you want me to stop.'

'Brandie, it's OK. I know your interest in becoming a healer is genuine . . . and I'm willing to do anything I can to help you on the way.'

'Bless you, Jude.' The reassurance had worked. Brandie grinned. 'I'll give you a call.'

'You do that.'

After Brandie had gone, Jude picked up the Dulux colour chart which she'd hidden under a cushion and set off.

She had already decided which colour she was going to have her sitting room painted, long before she talked to Carole or Brandie. Pale Sage. Dulux paint, readily available, didn't even need special mixing.

Brandie would not have disapproved. Green, after all – as she undoubtedly knew – was the colour corresponding with the fourth *chakra*, the Heart. Whose main issues were Love and Relationships. And the sense with which it was associated was Touch. What could be more appropriate for healing hands?

Footscrow House had had a great variety of incarnations. Originally a rectory, it had been built back in those Victorian days when the size of the clergyman's residence bore no relation to the size of his parish or congregation. At the time the foundation stone was laid, Fethering was little more than a fishing village. Though the fishermen and their families were dutiful churchgoers and appeared every week in their Sunday best, they only filled half the pews of All Saints Church. But that didn't reduce the scale on which the ten-bedroomed Footscrow House had been built. Clergymen of the time were notorious for having large families., as well as having a very comfortable lifestyle.

The building stayed in clerical occupancy until the early 1930s, when it was replaced by a smaller, rather drab new rectory further down the road. The next manifestation of the former rectory was as a boys' prep school, surviving until staff shortages caused by the Second World War forced the place to close. Footscrow House then remained empty and in a state of progressive dilapidation until the 1950s, when it became an 'approved school'. Since its pupils were what were then referred to as 'juvenile delinquents', it was certainly not approved of by the increasingly middle-class Fethering villagers. That incarnation closed, amidst unspecified and uninvestigated allegations of child abuse, in the late 1960s.

Thereafter, the building transmuted into – in no particular order – an upmarket restaurant, a drug rehabilitation centre (again not allowed to survive long by the censorious residents of Fethering), a boutique hotel, an alternative therapy spa, a care home, and the shrine of a cult led by the usual self-appointed and sexually voracious Messiah.

The one quality that all these enterprises had in common was complete lack of success. Nobody seemed able to make money out of Footscrow House. So much so that the building gained the local nickname of 'Fiasco House'.

That afternoon, when Jude went there to tell Pete the decorator about the colour choice for her sitting room, Fiasco House was in the process of being converted, by a local property developer called Roland Lasalle, into holiday flatlets.

As she approached the open front doors, a burly-looking elderly man came hurtling out of them. His hair and the beard on his prominent chin were steel-grey. A navy-blue polo shirt was stretched across his chubby but muscular torso. On its left-hand side was a yellow machine-embroidered logo, reading 'Lasalle Build and Design'. The man seemed preoccupied about something, angry perhaps. Certainly too caught up in his own affairs to notice Jude as he swept past her. He got into an open-backed truck parked outside, slamming the door, and driving off with something approaching fury.

On the side of the truck was painted the same logo. 'Lasalle Build and Design'.

Jude, always intrigued by human behaviour, idly wondered what had put the man's nose out of joint.

Like Jude, Pete must have been somewhere in his fifties. He'd been a decorator all his adult life, starting an apprenticeship straight out of school, working for local firms through his twenties into his early thirties when he set up on his own.

His high professional standards, honest charges and easy-going personality had built up a high reputation in the Fethering area. He didn't advertise in the local press or free sheets, his services weren't listed in the Yellow Pages, and he'd never bothered with social media or Checkatrade. His work came exclusively from personal recommendation. In a small community, word of mouth always trumps any amount of publicity.

Pete had worked on the inside and outside of many houses in Fethering. Some jobs had lasted less than a day, others weeks or even months. Owners had come to regard him as a welcome part of the furniture, an almost forgotten presence in their homes. And he'd got used to one job leading to another in the same house. Like most decorators, he had become accustomed to frequent requests beginning, 'Oh, while you're here . . .', 'Could you just . . .?' and 'Would it be possible for you to . . .?'

He was married with kids and his hobby was sailing. Never happier than when out on the water, he was a long-term stalwart of Fethering Yacht Club.

Pete was small and wiry but surprisingly strong. D-I-Y enthusiasts who spend any length of time up ladders soon realize the fitness required by being up one all day. Decorating involves a great deal of heavy lifting, moving beds and wardrobes to access the walls behind them. Every day is hard physical labour.

He had yellow-blond hair, showing no signs of greying, but beginning to thin from a growing circle of exposed skin at the back. His teeth were uneven, as though too many of them were trying to fit into his mouth. Throughout the year he wore paint-splattered overalls. The only thing that changed with the seasons was the number of garment layers beneath them.

It wasn't the first time Pete had worked on Footscrow House. Each new doomed incarnation of the place had involved a makeover, and he'd been employed in many of the more recent transitions. First under the aegis of Brenton Wilkinson, the owner of the firm he worked for as a young man, and later as an independent sole trader.

He had fixed with Jude that she could pop into the building that afternoon if she wanted to discuss colours. Then he could order the paint at the trade counter where he usually did business and be ready to start on Woodside Cottage Monday of the next week. He'd be working at Footscrow House till five, which was when he ended his working day, having usually started at eight in the morning. Though the building would be locked up at night, there was much toing and froing of other workmen during the day and Jude's appearance on the site would not be questioned.

Or maybe it would be simpler if she gave him a call when she was on her way and he could meet her downstairs . . .? They agreed to follow that plan.

Pete was waiting in the hall when she arrived and gave her a characteristic toothy grin. 'Hi, Jude.'

'Hi. You all right?'

A bigger grin. 'As ever.'

Before they could get into discussion of colours, they were interrupted by the appearance from one of the downstairs rooms of a tweed-suited, bustling man. Probably round fifty, reddish hair, shorter than average height, he carried a clipboard loaded with papers and an air of self-importance.

'Pete,' he said brusquely, 'I'm paying you to paint, not to stand around chatting up your girlfriends.'

Before the decorator had the opportunity to reply, the man had bustled out of the front door.

Jude could read in Pete's expression how much the words had hurt. In all the years he'd been employed round Fethering, nobody had ever questioned his work ethic.

'I'd better go up and get on,' he mumbled as he started for the stairs.

'I'll come with you,' said Jude.

He didn't object and she followed him silently up to the stripped-back room where he was working.

'Who was that charmer?' Jude asked.

'Roland Lasalle,' said Pete through clenched teeth. 'The developer behind this conversion.'

He didn't seem keen to say more. He picked up a hammer and chisel and returned to the job he must have been doing when he took her call, removing from the corner of the room a triangular plywood panel which had been painted over many times. The bedrooms had been divided up and opened out in many configurations over the years. In obedience to the architects of the moment, irregular spaces and alcoves had been created and covered over in a fairly haphazard way. The room they were now in was large, indicating that the new holiday flatlets were being planned on a generous scale.

The way he wielded his hammer suggested how much Pete was still smarting from the accusation of skiving. He had never skived in his life.

A couple more over-vigorous blows from the hammer, a couple more pulls on the wedged-in chisel, and the panel came loose. He grabbed the corner and worked the cover free from its fixing nails. Through a cloud of dust, a small triangular alcove was revealed. Pete peered inside.

'Blimey O'Reilly!' he said. 'I wonder how long that's been there . . .?'

TWO

It was a handbag.

A woman's red leather bucket bag, which might have been in fashion some twenty or thirty years previously. It certainly wore a coating of twenty or thirty years' dust.

Pete and Jude exchanged looks. Surprise had now replaced hurt in his expression. 'Well,' she said, 'there's no way that was left there accidentally.'

'How do you know?'

'Because I'm a woman, Pete. The relationship between a woman and her handbag, even in these more enlightened days, is akin to that between Siamese twins. If you carry one, you never want to let it out of your sight. There is no way the handbag's owner could have just left it in this alcove by mistake.'

'Equally,' said Pete, 'there's no way whoever boarded this in and painted over it didn't know that the handbag was there.'

'Hm.' Jude was silent for a moment. Her instinct was to reach for the bag and check its contents, but a strange voice inside her head said she shouldn't touch anything at a crime scene. Which was, of course, complete nonsense. There was no crime involved. She and Pete had just found a handbag. She reached forward for it.

If it had been a crime scene, the police would have now possessed some very fine examples of Jude's fingerprints. The dull leather was furry with dust.

The zip across the top was stiff but not rusted. She eased it open and examined the contents. No mobile phone from back then, obviously. Lipstick, a powder compact, a packet of tissues, some small change. In fact, only one thing that might have been unexpected in a woman's handbag. A blue UK passport.

Jude opened it. Though dusty, the passport looked new, its pages unmarked by any stamps. The photograph was of a blonde woman with glasses. In her early twenties. She looked a little embarrassed at having her picture taken.

The name of the passport owner was Anita Garner.

Intriguing though it was, their discovery was basically just a woman's handbag. Pete said he'd try to find out when the closing-off of the alcove might have happened. Brenton Wilkinson, the decorator he had originally worked for (now long retired), had been involved in many of the transformations of Footscrow House. The old man might be able to put a date on it. Assuming, of course, he'd still got all his marbles. Brenton Wilkinson had been in a local authority care home for some years.

Meanwhile, Jude, conscious of the importance of a lost handbag to any woman, even after twenty or thirty years, decided that she should take it to the police. Whether they would still have records of a reported missing handbag from so long ago was not really her concern. She just knew that handing the bag in was the right thing to do.

Before she delivered it, though – and she didn't know quite why but her instinct told her to – she made a note of the document's issue date and its owner's personal details.

Fethering's police station was a small building, only open during office hours. It operated as a kind of branch office for the bigger set-up in Fedborough.

The uniformed constable behind the reception desk took possession of the handbag and noted the circumstances of how it had been found. He also took Jude's contact details. While unfailingly polite, he still managed to give the impression that finding the handbag's owner was not high on his list of priorities. He was more interested in real crime.

And he was too young to know the extent to which the passport-owner's name and crime had once been associated in the prurient minds of Fethering.

'Anita Garner,' echoed Carole. 'It does ring a distant bell.'

'Did you know her?'

'No, she wasn't in Fethering when we first came here.' The 'we' was a rare giveaway. After their divorce, Carole had expunged from her life all reference to her ex-husband David.

They had bought High Tor as a couple, a weekend place to give their son Stephen a bit of seaside time when he was young. But his parents had parted long before Carole – when she retired from the Home Office – had moved to Fethering full time.

'So, how do you know the name?'

Behind their rimless glasses, Carole's pale blue eyes screwed up in puzzlement. 'It must have been from hearing people talk about her, I suppose. Some mystery . . .? Maybe she disappeared . . .? I've a feeling it was something like that. I'll do some research,' she concluded firmly.

'Excellent,' said Jude. Carole was very good at research.

Jude wasn't as regular as her neighbour in her walking habits. Carole, under the pretence that it was her Labrador Gulliver rather than she who needed an unchanging structure to the day, was on Fethering Beach with him before seven on summer mornings and as soon as it got light in the winter. Gulliver also got another brisk constitutional and toilet break in the early evening.

Jude was more random in all of her habits. The generous nature of her curves, under their usual drapes of skirts, tops and scarves, suggested a relaxed fitness and dietary regime. Her attitude to many things in her life was relaxed. She thought being alive was a natural state of affairs, an attitude her neighbour could never quite embrace.

So, Jude didn't go for a walk when she felt she ought to go for a walk, she walked when she felt like walking. And the next morning, the Thursday, she felt like a walk on Fethering Beach. She had a couple of clients booked in for the afternoon but nothing till then. So, she wrapped herself in a variety of warming layers of wool and set out.

For some reason, her thoughts were still browsing on the discovery of Anita Garner's handbag. The oddity of it got to her. The act of concealment was so deliberate. For Jude, whose whole life was a quest for understanding human behaviour, an explanation was required.

Some of West Sussex's seaside towns are big on beach huts. Brighton, Hove, Worthing and Littlehampton have great parades of them. Carole once rented one to entertain a visiting grandchild in Smalting, a little way along the coast from Fethering. And though they don't command the astronomical prices of the ones in Bournemouth and Sandbanks, some West Sussex beach huts are very sought after. There are always long waiting lists of people eager to buy them.

Fethering, however, didn't compete on that level. There were a few beach huts at the edge of the dunes furthest away from the mouth of the River Fether, just before the exclusive Shorelands Estate, whose most favoured properties had grounds which gave direct access to the beach.

Before walkers reached these back garden walls, they would come across an uneven row of half a dozen beach huts. They weren't built to standard local authority specifications, not identical structures in rows like the yellow, blue and green ones at Littlehampton's East Beach. They had been put up randomly over the years. One was an Edwardian wooden structure that would not have looked out of place in a Chekhov play, another looked like a cricket pavilion, while the rest had been put up without the advice of an architect. None really deserved to be in the category of 'hut'. They were much more upmarket and spacious than that.

They also dated from a time before certain nitpicking restrictions had been imposed by Fether District Council. More recently built beach huts were forbidden from having electrical power or plumbing. On some beaches, under sufferance, barbecues were allowed, but basically nothing was permitted that might extend a day's stay overnight. That was a rule that was strictly policed by the local authority. The nice middle-class people of the South Coast were paranoid about their empty spaces being commandeered by 'travellers', illegal immigrants and what they saw as other freeloaders. They distrusted all outsiders and assumed that their countryside and shoreline should be the exclusive preserve of people like them.

The old huts on Fethering Beach, however, had been put up long before such strictures and so retained their ancient rights to power and plumbing. Nights could be spent in them with impunity. And their owners were rich enough to conform to Fethering's standards of respectability.

As Jude walked towards the huts, she saw ahead of her someone she knew. The woman's name was Lauren Givens. 'Knew' was in the Fethering sense of the word. Which meant that each woman knew the other by name, they knew a certain amount about each other's background but hadn't spent any length of time in each other's company. On passing such an acquaintance on the beach, Carole would have vouchsafed a curt and silent 'Fethering nod'. Jude, having a more expansive personality, upgraded this, as she overtook the woman, to a beaming smile and a 'Good morning'.

Lauren Givens's reaction was unusual. She can't have heard Jude's approach, because she turned towards her as in shock at the greeting. She had been slowing down, possibly to go to one of the beach huts, but now, with a flustered, 'Oh, hello', she stood still for an uncertain moment. Then, clapping her hand on the empty back pocket of her jeans, she announced, 'Oh damn, I've left my phone at home', and set off smartly back towards the village.

The moment she had turned around, the heavens suddenly opened, with a deluge of icy February rain.

Oh dear. Amongst the voluminous woollen layers Jude had wrapped herself in that morning, none was even mildly waterproof. And she didn't have an umbrella with her. There was no point in hurrying to minimize her exposure to the rain. She reconciled herself to arriving back at Woodside Cottage in a totally sodden state.

Ahead of her on the beach, Lauren Givens had made a different calculation. She clearly reckoned running would get her home quicker, back into the dry. And her running seemed somehow a continuation of the furtiveness she had demonstrated when surprised by Jude.

As the first discomforting drips trickled down between her collar and her back, Jude idly wondered why Lauren Givens had reacted like that. She sieved her brain for the little she knew about the woman. Some kind of artist, she recollected . . . well, perhaps a craftswoman would be nearer the mark. Made little ceramic toadstools and 'collectibles', which sold in gift shops along the South Coast.

Not in quantities to make a living from, but Jude seemed to recall there was a rich husband in the background. Couldn't remember his name, didn't even know that she'd ever heard it. Some job in international marketing . . .? Member of Fethering

Yacht Club . . .? He stayed in London most of the week, while his wife was a permanent Fethering resident. Oh yes, and there had been a flyer through the letterbox recently about a Pottery Open Day that Lauren was hosting in her studio the following Wednesday.

But that was the sum total of the local gossip Jude had heard about the couple.

Fortunately, she hadn't left *her* phone at home. Because at that moment it rang.

The police station in Fedborough. Would it be convenient for them to call on her at home around four that afternoon? They wanted to ask for more detail about the circumstances of her finding Anita Garner's handbag.

Carole's relationship with her laptop was typical of most of her relationships. She had started from a position of distrust and scepticism. Like anything else new, this new technology couldn't be healthy. Engaging with it would be tantamount to signing up to a Faustian pact. The small advantages the laptop brought would come at a terrible cost. It was safer not to get involved.

Then, gradually, she began to feel a little isolated without access to email. Everyone else seemed to have it, even people considerably older than she was, people she might have consigned to the ungenerous category of 'fuddy-duddies'. Carole Seddon's main aim in life was to pass unnoticed under the radar, but there came a point when not having email drew more attention to her as a non-conforming oddity. Then there was all that information available at the click of a mouse. And Carole loved information.

Even better, from Carole Seddon's point of view, owning a laptop offered the possibility of doing one's shopping without having to talk to anyone.

Needless to say, she didn't advertise the fact that she was intending to join the information technology revolution. After much private reading-up on the subject, she paid a clandestine visit to PC World in Clincham and quickly made her purchase. She then, rather than leaving her neat Renault in front of High Tor as usual, parked it back in the garage, smuggling her new possession into the house unseen.

It was only after two intense weeks of familiarizing herself with the technology that she casually mentioned to Jude that she'd bought a laptop.

And from that moment on, the relationship between woman and machine had been intense. The only anomaly about it was that Carole did not acknowledge the laptop's portability. Her keyboard activities almost always took place in the spare bedroom. Everything had an allocated space in the circumscribed life of High Tor, and that was the computer room. The miniaturizing achievements of Silicon Valley geniuses in breaking away from the cumbersome behemoths of previous generations were wasted on Carole Seddon. She used her laptop like a desktop.

So, it was in her spare room that she began her research into the life of Anita Garner. She started with Google. There were a surprising number of people referenced as 'Anita Garner' or close variations of the name. A paediatrician in Napier New Zealand, a vocalist with grunge revival band of the 1990s who hailed from Little Rock Arkansas, an event caterer from Porthcawl in Wales . . . None of them seemed to have any connection with Fethering.

Which meant that Carole had to focus her research more locally. She remembered that amongst the limited facilities of the village library was a complete bound set of copies of the *Fethering Observer*, since its first appearance in 1893.

Leaving a reproachful Gulliver by the Aga – he'd quickly deduced that he wasn't going to get a bonus walk – Carole set off to investigate.

The police – one male, one female, both in uniform – arrived on the dot of four at Woodside Cottage. They did not stay long and Jude rather wondered why they'd bothered to come at all. She had been unable to add much to what she had told the desk sergeant the day before. And her visitors seemed to accept the unlikelihood of her having anything to do with the woman whose handbag had been immured long before Jude had moved to Fethering.

The detail they did seem interested in – and indeed asked her repeated questions about – was Pete's reaction to the discovery. Had he been surprised to find the handbag?

Jude replied that he'd been no more surprised than anyone

who found a long-abandoned handbag behind a wooden panel
would be.

'Did he react as if he expected to find a handbag there?'

'No, of course he didn't.'

And that was it, really. The female officer took copious notes
of their conversation. Maybe their interview was just to get the
paperwork sorted. There had been many complaints within
the Force about increasing amounts of paperwork.

Jude saw them politely to her front door. They thought it
unlikely they'd need to ask her any further questions.

Carole's reluctance to acknowledge her laptop's portability meant
that she had not taken it with her to Fethering Library. So, all
the research she did there had been written longhand into a
notebook. Data which she would later copy on to her laptop in
the spare/computer room. Despite her self-appointed reputation
for efficiency, something which carried through from her time at
the Home Office, Carole Seddon did not always take the direct
route to her destinations.

But she couldn't wait for the transcribing process to be
completed to share her findings. The moment she got back to
High Tor, pausing only to print out something from her laptop,
she was on the phone to Woodside Cottage. (Most people would
just have knocked on their neighbour's front door as she passed,
but that was never Carole Seddon's way. To her mind, that kind
of casual 'dropping-in' was associated with people from the
North. People who viewed – and lived the life of – *Coronation
Street*, a programme which she had never watched.) Of course,
when she got through to Jude, she received the anticipated invitation to go next door, where her neighbour had just opened a
bottle of New Zealand Sauvignon Blanc.

With their glasses charged and the first grateful slurp slurped,
Carole embarked on her revelations.

'Anita Garner used to live in Fethering. She went missing
about thirty years ago. Her disappearance got brief coverage in
the national press and quite a lot more in the *Fethering Observer*.
I've been going through their files.'

'Online?'

'No, they aren't online.' If they had been online, Carole would have felt rather disappointed. Research ought to involve hard work. 'I've been going through the archives at Fethering Library.'

'Good for you.'

With a flourish, Carole produced the sheet that she had just printed out. (Of course, if she'd brought the laptop with her, she could just have shown the image on the screen, but that was never her way.) It was a photograph, taken from a newspaper, of Anita Garner. Jude recognized her instantly from the image she'd seen in the passport. In this one, though, the subject wasn't wearing her glasses and looked quite a bit more glamorous. And dated – her blonde hair was long and chunky in the haystack style of Jennifer Anniston from *Friends*. It suggested a posed picture, taken by a professional photographer, the kind of thing that parents might display proudly on their mantelpieces. Typical of the images that turn up in the press when someone goes missing, images that seem somehow firmly to suggest the person is already dead.

Carole was silent. Jude knew she wanted the satisfaction of actually being asked for information. She always relished playing a scene at her own pace.

Jude readily conceded. 'So, what have you found out?' she asked.

The answer came in a rush. Now unleashed, Carole had so much to tell. 'Anita Garner was twenty-three when she disappeared. At the time she was actually working at Footscrow House. It was a care home back then. She had started helping in the kitchens but was training to become a qualified carer. She was an only child, brought up in Fethering, as I said. On the Downside Estate. She had left school at sixteen to attend a catering college, though there was some suggestion she didn't finish the course there. Before she went to the care home, she worked in the hospitality industry, chambermaiding in hotels, behind the bar in pubs, also helping out in the kitchens. All of her work was local – Fethering, Fedborough, Smalting, not much further afield than that. At the time of her disappearance, she was still living at home with her parents in the house where she was born.'

Carole's need to take a breath gave Jude the opportunity to ask, 'Had she ever worked abroad?'

'Not so far as I could find out, no.'

'Had she ever travelled abroad?'

'I don't know,' said Carole a little peevishly. She didn't like any criticism of her information hoard. 'Newspapers don't tell everything about a person.'

'No, of course they don't. I just thought . . . the fact that there was a passport in her handbag . . .'

'Anyway, the library closed at five.' Carole still sounded defensive. 'It took me a long time to find the right editions of the *Fethering Observer* to get started. I haven't seen everything. I'm planning to go back tomorrow.'

'It's great how much you have managed to find out,' said Jude, smoothing ruffled feathers, not for the first time.

'There was a lot of speculation in the press about what might have happened to her.'

That was inevitable in a village like Fethering, where the two-day absence of a cat could qualify as front-page news.

'Some people thought,' Carole went on, 'she might have been the victim of a serial killer. A character dubbed by the press "The Brighton Batterer" had been linked to a series of murders over a few years. But Anita Garner's profile didn't seem to fit. The Batterer's victims had all been prostitutes and there was really no solid proof that the killings were the work of the same man. Whoever he was – or whoever they were – the police never found him – or them. But the rumours about the killer caused some years of anxiety for women in Brighton.

'Then again, there were the usual suggestions Anita Garner might have been kidnapped by sex traffickers, Russian agents, Islamic terrorists – Fethering's usual suspects all lined up.

'The girl's parents were interviewed time and again. Was she unhappy at home? No. Had her behaviour ever given her parents cause for concern? No, she was a good Catholic girl, went to Mass every Sunday. Had she just broken up a relationship? Was she in a relationship? No and no.

'Then the more desperate question . . . Did Anita have any enemies? Anyone who might have borne a grudge from school-days? All the answers still negative.'

Jude looked thoughtful. 'Do you know if her parents are still alive?'

'No. Her father went relatively soon after the disappearance. Big Catholic funeral at Fedborough Abbey, apparently. Her mother died about ten years ago.'

'Mm. Mind you, there'd be a lot of other Fethering locals still here from that time. As you know, Carole, it doesn't take much to get the gossip-mills turning in a place like this.'

'Very true.' The pale blue eyes sparkled, attracted by the idea of a 'case' to investigate. 'So, where do you suggest we start?'

'We start by finding out as much local gossip as we can about Anita Garner.' Jude looked at her big round watch. 'Do you know . . . I could fancy another drink . . . at the Crown and Anchor.'

THREE

'She was definitely murdered,' Barney Poulton pontificated. 'If the police were to do a really thorough search of the South Downs, I guarantee they'd find Anita Garner's bones. In a shallow grave. That is, if the foxes hadn't got to it. Then the bones might be more scattered.'

Carole and Jude exchanged looks. Barney Poulton, that day dressed in a navy guernsey sweater above burgundy corduroys, was almost a fixture in the Crown and Anchor these days. Summer visitors, encountering him for the first time in the bar, took him for a genuine local, 'the eyes and ears of the village', the source of endless recollection and regional lore. Many drinks were bought for him on the premise of his authenticity. He was the self-appointed Sage of Fethering.

So convincingly did he fill the role that newcomers would assume him to be village born and bred, and rarely to have stirred outside his birthplace.

They couldn't have been more wrong. As Carole and Jude knew well, Barney Poulton had retired to Fethering relatively recently, having spent his working life commuting daily from Walton-on-Thames to a solicitor's practice in London. But that didn't stop him from expounding on every local issue.

He did this, much to the annoyance of Ted Crisp, the bearded, unkempt and unreconstructed landlord of the Crown and Anchor, who, at the pub's quiet times, provided the only audience for Barney's endless ruminations. Boring local regulars are among the enduring hazards of running a pub. Sometimes Ted wished he'd followed the example of a publican friend of his who'd put up over his end of the bar a notice reading: 'NO SYMPATHY CORNER'.

Fortunately, that early evening, Ted did not have to face the monologue alone. Apart from Carole and Jude, there were a few other regulars in the bar, all of whom, in the Fethering way, the two women knew by name, though they'd never spent much time with them. They were people who, on encounter in the village, would have received a 'Fethering nod' from Carole and a beaming vocal greeting from Jude.

But there was an elderly couple in the pub that evening whom Jude knew a bit better. They were sitting in one of the alcoves, finishing an early fish-and-chips supper, each making a modest half of bitter last the meal. Leslie and Vi Benyon, both in their eighties. Vi had the comfortable contours of a cottage loaf. Leslie, by contrast, was stick thin. In fact, they reminded Jude of a long-remembered illustration from a childhood book of nursery rhymes. Jack Spratt and his wife; he eating no fat, she no lean.

She had met them when their grown-up daughter had contacted her about her father's insomnia. Leslie was one of those clients with whom Jude reckoned she was never going to make any headway. He could have matched Carole for scepticism about the whole business of healing. Paying for a healer's services made as much sense to him as 'backing a three-legged horse in the Derby'.

But his daughter, who had herself benefited from Jude's ministrations for a problem of low self-esteem, managed to persuade him to have one session, which she would pay for. The deal was that, if he didn't think it'd done any good, they'd give up the idea. If he felt any benefit at all, his daughter would pay for a second appointment.

When he first arrived in the sitting room of Woodside Cottage, Leslie Benyon's whole body expressed distrust and disbelief. It was almost like a smell rising off him. He stated stoutly that he refused to take any clothes off (Jude hadn't asked him to) and was deeply reluctant to lie on her treatment bed.

So she, knowing well that different clients required different approaches, stopped persuading him to do anything, sat him in an armchair and offered him a cup of tea. She was a good listener and expert at drawing out secrets. This was not a skill that she had worked on. Jude was just genuinely interested in other people.

Leslie Benyon, it turned out, had been a military man, and it soon became clear to her that events he had witnessed in Northern Ireland had destroyed his mental equilibrium. He had a soldier's reticence, a gruff unwillingness to burden others with his troubles. 'I couldn't talk to Vi about it. Nothing that happened out there was her fault, after all, was it?'

No healing took place at that encounter. Jude's hands did not venture near any part of his body. But she was extremely gratified when, a week later, Leslie's daughter rang to say he wanted to take up her offer of a second paid-for session.

And, after some months of healing (which he was then happy to pay for himself), Leslie's sleep patterns returned to a kind of normal.

That evening in the Crown and Anchor, Jude did not expect more than 'a Fethering nod' from him. In the presence of his wife, Leslie was still embarrassed about the dealings he had had with her. Or perhaps the fact that he'd needed to have dealings with her. With Vi, he needed to maintain his strong, silent persona.

This was no hardship to his wife. It was probably the way their marriage had worked from the start – he the quiet observant one, she the talker. And Vi was certainly garrulous. Which, from the point of view of Carole and Jude's fact-finding mission, was rather convenient. Because the conversation in the Crown and Anchor was about Anita Garner.

How that had happened was just another of those Fethering mysteries. Neither Carole nor Jude had mentioned the woman's name. The discovery of the handbag at Footscrow House was, so far as they knew, only known to the two of them, Pete the decorator and the police at Fethering and Fedborough. And yet, within hours, Anita Garner was once again being discussed in the Crown and Anchor. Carole and Jude no longer allowed themselves to wonder at the speed and efficiency of the Fethering bush telegraph.

'There was a lot of talk when that Anita disappeared,' Vi Benyon remarked to fill the momentary silence while Barney Poulton was preparing his next baseless conjecture.

Jude was quick enough to detect the slight shake of the head that Leslie directed towards his wife, but Vi, either not seeing or ignoring the admonition, went on, 'Fiasco House was a care home back then . . . not, from all accounts, a very good one. Anita Garner worked there.'

'Did you know her?' asked Jude.

'Ooh, known her from way back. She went through school with our boy Kent. A bunch of them was always going around together, them and Glen Porter and a few others. Well, they was mates at the primary, but when they all go to the comprehensive, suddenly the boys didn't want to be seen around girls.' She chuckled. 'And, a few years later, they want to be all over them, you know, like young people do.

'Anyway, Kent never had a lot to do with Anita after school, but he knew her. He was as surprised as anyone when she disappeared. Lots of talk there was round Fethering back then about what might have happened to her.'

'Yes, well, Vi, I don't think we need to revive any of that again now, do we?' said Leslie Benyon.

But his wife was not to be put off her stride. 'Didn't last much longer as a care home after that,' she went on. 'There was talk locally about things having gone seriously wrong there. Old people being maltreated, you know.'

'Was there an official inquiry?' asked Carole, who liked everything to be official.

'Don't know about that,' Vi replied. 'But, as I say, a lot of talk locally.'

'Was the talk,' asked Jude, 'about Anita Garner being involved in the maltreatment of patients?'

'No, no. Not that. Suggestion was more that she might have seen some bad stuff going on and reported it . . . you know, like a . . . what's the word?'

'"Whistle-blower"?' Jude suggested.

'That's it, yes. "Whistle-blower".' She repeated the word, savouring it. 'There was people round Fethering at the time reckoned that was what happened.'

'There was people round Fethering at the time,' said Leslie Benyon harshly, 'who reckoned all kinds of other things happened, and all. And none of it was ever any more than gossip. As it always is round here.'

But if he thought that would finally silence his wife, he was wrong. Much to the satisfaction of Carole and Jude, Vi continued, 'I think what I just said was a lot more believable than most of the other stuff there was around back then. All that business about Anita having had affairs with people. The nonsense they talked. She was a quiet, well-behaved girl from a good Catholic family. But, the way people went on about it, you'd have thought she'd had it off with everyone in Fethering who wore trousers.'

Leslie Benyon stirred himself as if about to rise from their alcove, but Jude managed to get her question in quick enough. 'Do you know of anyone who Anita actually did have a relationship with?'

'Not for certain, no,' the old woman replied. 'Well, Glen Porter said he'd had a thing with her, but then he claimed back then he'd been inside every pair of knickers in Fethering.'

This time Leslie really had had enough. Rising briskly, he announced, 'Time we were off, Vi.'

She didn't argue. With muttered goodbyes, the couple left the Crown and Anchor.

Jude looked up at Ted Crisp behind the bar. 'Glen Porter? You know him?'

'Know who is. Not a regular. He's one of the bunch who do their drinking at Fethering Yacht Club. Rarely comes in here.'

'Oh, *I* know him.' The speaker was, inevitably, Barney Poulton. He, of course, knew everything about Fethering, far more than the people who'd lived in the village twenty times longer than he had. 'We play golf together.'

Jude caught a perfect snapshot of Ted's reaction to this. Behind its shaggy hair and beard, his expression summed up a whole catalogue of thought. The first was: Of course, you bloody would know Glen Porter. Then: And I know you play golf – you bloody go on about it enough. Finally, a plea: So, why don't you hang around the golf club bar – which is, after all, the natural habitat for bores – boring everyone to tears in there, rather than in my bloody pub?

'What does Glen Porter do?' asked Carole. 'I haven't heard of him.' Which, in Fethering, was unusual.

'He doesn't do anything,' Barney replied. 'Lucky bugger. Hasn't done anything for decades. Still way below retirement age.'

'He inherited money, didn't he?' said Ted.

But Barney Poulton didn't want outside contributors to his

narrative. As if the landlord hadn't spoken, he went on, 'Glen had a very rich uncle, called Reefer Townsend. Don't know how he got the name. He was a widower . . . we must be talking thirty years ago now . . . and his son was lined up to inherit everything. Son suddenly dies – and Glen cops the lot.'

'How did the son die?' asked Carole, antennae instantly aflicker.

'Don't know that,' Barney was forced to admit, a little miffed at having his image of omniscience dented. 'Anyway, since school Glen had been doing odd jobs locally, behind bars, stacking shelves, portering in hospitals and care homes, nothing permanent. Suddenly, out of the blue, he inherits Reefer Townsend's big house up on the Downs beyond Fedborough, beach hut here in Fethering, and enough in investments to ensure he never has to work again. All he has to do for the rest of his life is to splash the cash, live the life of a playboy. Very nice, thank you.'

'Strange, that I've never even heard the name,' Carole persisted. 'Has he moved away from the area?'

'No, still keeps the house – and the beach hut. Travels a lot, though . . . South Africa . . . Caribbean . . . Mexico . . . you name it. All right for some, eh?'

Barney Poulton looked at his watch. 'Anyway, I can't sit here gossiping all day.'

Jude caught another snapshot of Ted Crisp's face, which read: Well, you bloody *seem* to be able to.

'Must get back home,' Barney went on as he rose from his bar stool. 'Don't want a rocket from Her Indoors, do I?'

Ted Crisp's face expressed the fervent wish that Her Indoors would provide a constant supply of rockets – ideally armed with nuclear warheads – or anything else that would keep her husband out of the Crown and Anchor.

But he didn't say anything. He didn't need to. Carole and Jude intuited what he was feeling.

'Incidentally, Ted,' asked Jude, once the unwelcome regular had departed, 'have you come across a guy called Roland Lasalle?'

'Sure have. He's a waste of space if ever there was one.'

'Oh?' Both women had great faith in Ted's judgement when it came to the locals.

'*Roland*' – he put a snide, upper-class accent on the word – 'is the prime example of First Generation Posh.' They waited for elaboration. 'His parents are Harry and Veronica Lasalle. He's a local builder, Harry. Good at his job but, know what I mean, no pretensions. Made pots of money over the years and he – or I think probably more *she* – invested a lot of it into private education for her precious Roland. Almost did too good a job, Veronica. Turned the boy into someone so posh he hardly acknowledges his own parents.'

The description fitted the bad-tempered man Jude had heard being so offensive to Pete. If ever she'd met someone with a sense of entitlement, he'd fitted the bill.

'Well, you know the old saying: You can polish a . . .' Ted had been planning a stronger word but checked himself to come up with a more acceptable alternative – 'piece of dirt, but that doesn't stop it from being a piece of dirt.'

'And is Roland Lasalle,' asked Jude, 'involved in what's currently going on down at Footscrow House?'

'"Involved"? You could say that. Only his project, isn't it? Dad's a builder, but *Roland*' – the same dismissive intonation – 'can't get his fingers dirty with cement and sawdust, can he? Not with his university degree and architectural qualification. No, Roland Lasalle's a property developer now, isn't he? Hoping to clean up when the holiday flatlets are finished. Mind you, if this caper follows the pattern of everything else that's happened to Fiasco House . . .' Ted Crisp didn't need to complete the sentence.

'Is it his own money he's putting into the project?' asked Carole, always shrewder than her neighbour on questions like that.

The landlord shrugged. 'Who knows? Bit of his own, maybe. I'd've thought he'd got backers, though – sure to have. His old man might be involved. Harry's not short of a few bob. If Roland had asked Veronica to twist his arm, the old boy wouldn't have said no.'

'Sounds like she wears the trousers in that household,' Carole observed.

'And how! Poor Harry has to get permission before he can . . .' another hastily decorous substitution – 'go to the toilet.'

'Well, I had my first encounter with Roland Lasalle recently,' said Jude.

'Oh, yes?'

'Down at Footscrow House . . .'

'Yeah?'

'. . . where he was bawling out Pete the decorator.'

'Bawling out Pete?' The landlord looked as affronted as if he himself had been bawled out. 'But no one has a bad word to say about Pete.'

'Roland Lasalle did.'

'Typical.' Ted swept a hand up through his matted hair. 'Proves my point, I'd say.'

Carole was curious. 'You say his father's a builder?'

'*Was* a builder. Pretty well retired now, I think. His back's knackered.'

'Would he be involved in the current work on Footscrow House?'

'Bound to be. Probably not hands-on, but his company will be in on it. Lasalle Build and Design. Harry's had a hand in virtually every other renovation of Fiasco House.'

'Then I wonder if, back when it was a care home—?'

But Carole's incipient investigation was cut short by the arrival in the bar of a newcomer, who came straight towards the two women.

'Brandie!' Jude announced.

'You said you might be in here later.'

'Which, as you see, I am.' Jude gestured towards her neighbour. 'This is my friend, Carole. Brandie.'

'Brandie?' The echo contained Carole's disbelief that the word could actually be a name.

'Drinks,' said Jude hastily. 'Sauvignon Blanc right for you, Brandie?'

'Fab.'

Ignoring Carole's wince, Jude said, 'I'll get us refills too,' and made for the bar before her neighbour could remonstrate that she didn't need any more. Or that she only wanted a small one.

While Jude went to order, Brandie turned to Carole. 'Have you been a friend of Jude's for a long time?'

'Long enough.' She meant it as a casual reply, not realizing

that the words could sound as though she did not wish the relationship to continue. Throughout her life, Carole had had a
propensity for unwittingly making remarks like that, which made
her appear more combative than she really was (though, it has
to be said, she was already quite combative).

'Oh. And are you part of the healing community?'

Had she been searching for two words to antagonize her
listener, Brandie could not have made a more accurate selection.
Healing? Well, Carole's views on that were very clear. And she
had frequently expressed her distrust of any phrase that began
with the word 'community'.

'No, I am not,' she replied icily. 'Friendship does not imply
a shared belief in mumbo-jumbo.'

As she returned with the drinks, Jude was aware of the silence,
not to say '*froideur*'. Oh dear, she thought. As she could have
anticipated, Carole and Brandie was never going to be a marriage
made in heaven, was it?

FOUR

Jude liked to keep leisurely hours. Quite capable of getting up for an early appointment when required, she preferred a routine incorporating a cup of tea made in the kitchen and enjoyed back upstairs. Her perfect way of greeting the day was from under the duvet. The residents of the adjacent High Tor, woman and dog, would, on an ideal day, have returned from their brisk walk on Fethering Beach long before their neighbour had started to think about getting dressed.

But the following morning, the Friday, Jude's laze was interrupted by the telephone ringing. The caller, to her surprise, was Vi Benyon. 'Sorry, Jude, to trouble you so early, but I wanted to talk to you while Leslie's out walking the dog.'

These words instantly shifted Jude from comatose to fully alert. 'Oh, yes? What was it about?'

The answer could not have been better. 'Well, you know last night we were talking about Anita Garner . . .?'

'Yes?' said Jude eagerly.

'There were things I could have said then, but I didn't because Leslie didn't want me to.'

Even better. Jude reckoned Vi didn't need another prompt.

She was proved right as the words tumbled out of the old woman's mouth. 'The fact is, I always felt unhappy about what happened to Anita. I mean, people don't just vanish off the face of the earth, do they? She must've gone somewhere, and I didn't reckon the police took her disappearance seriously enough. It was as if nobody cared about the girl.'

'My friend Carole found quite a lot of coverage of her disappearance in back copies of the *Fethering Observer*.'

'Oh yes, there was a lot of fuss at the time, but people soon forget. Fethering's always been a hotbed for gossip' – You don't have to tell me that, thought Jude – 'but the local attention span is short.'

Perhaps now a nudge was needed. 'Vi, do you actually know something specific about what happened to Anita?'

'Not exactly, no. But she was working at Footscrow House which, back then, was a care home . . .'

'I'd heard that, yes.'

'. . . and my mother was a resident there at the time.'

'Really?'

'Terrible place, I'm sorry to say. Standards of care, particularly considering the money they were charging, they was terrible. My mum would be calling for hours for a carer to come and help her . . . and when one eventually did come, they couldn't speak English. And she was like as not to get a man as a woman . . . which was undignified for a lady of Mum's generation. She wasn't used to having men dealing with her . . . private needs.'

Jude was beginning to think another nudge might be required to shift Vi Benyon off the familiar track of the inadequacy of care homes, but the old woman reined herself in.

'Anyway, Mum knew Anita Garner. She was one of the few carers who she actually liked . . . who actually *cared*, you could say. Kind girl, seemed genuinely interested in an old biddy's reminiscences. And I'm not saying my mum wasn't a talker, but she had lots to talk about. Well, Anita had lived her whole life around Fethering, so she knew the places and some of the people Mum talked about. And what's more . . .' Vi Benyon held the pause like a professional storyteller – 'Anita told her some of the stuff that was going on behind the scenes at Footscrow House.'

'Like what?' asked Jude eagerly.

'Well, there was . . . This is all rather difficult for me, because when Anita disappeared, it was round the time my mum was on the way out, so I was preoccupied with that. You know, her final illness and passing, the funeral and family complications . . . And I loved my mum to bits, so I wasn't in a good state. Otherwise, I might have followed up more on some of the stuff Anita told me.'

Jude managed to restrain herself from demanding what Anita *did* actually tell her, and fortunately Vi continued, 'Apparently, the standards of cleanliness at Footscrow House, you know, back when it was a care home, was really terrible. I wish I'd known more about it before I put Mum in there. I might have looked somewhere else, though there wasn't much available, not on the budget we had. But standards there was very low. Sheets not changed nearly as often as they should have been, mice in the kitchen, you name it. No surprise the place was closed down fairly soon afterwards.

'But, according to Anita, this level of neglect wasn't down to the carers being slack or anything like that. It was management policy. The staff was effectively told to lower their standards. Well, it was to save money, wasn't it? Save on the laundry bills. There are always people who're ready to cut corners if it's going to save them a few bob, aren't there?'

'Too true. Sadly.' Jude was still hoping for something more specific. 'Did Anita Garner actually have any run-ins with the management? You suggested when we were in the Crown and Anchor that she might have complained to them about the way things were being run?'

'Yes, being one of those . . . oh, what's the word? Tell me again.'

'"Whistle-blowers"?'

'I can never get that right. But, yes, Mum said she thought Anita had complained. But I don't know whether the girl got into trouble over that. I'm sure the management wouldn't have liked it, though.' Vi Benyon was silent for a moment, and Jude was worried she might have said her piece. But then the old woman resumed, 'No, the problems Anita had at Footscrow House back then were more . . . personal.'

'How do you mean?'

'Well, there was someone at the care home who kept . . . you know . . . coming on to her.'

'Oh? Did she say who that person was?'

'She did give me a name' – Vi hesitated – 'but I'm not sure that I should mention it . . .'

'Oh, come on,' Jude urged her. 'That could be important. It might well have something to do with why Anita disappeared.'

'Yes, it might. I'd thought that at the time. And there was a bit of gossip round Fethering about the possibility.'

Another silence. Then an abrupt 'Oh, here's Leslie back with the dog.'

And Vi Benyon ended the call.

Leaving Jude in a state of considerable frustration.

Fethering Library was not of a size to have a separate room for archival research. The bound copies of the *Fethering Observer* were kept in a large metal cupboard which had to be unlocked by the librarian Di Thompson. For reasons of space on the available tables, Carole was only allowed to take out four volumes at a time. Then the cupboard had to be locked again until she had finished with those four. Whereupon the processes of unlocking and retrieving had to be repeated. That was how access had always been arranged, and that was how it continued to be arranged.

It was Carole's view that this level of security was unnecessary. Had the cupboard contained copies of Shakespeare's First Folio, there might have been some point. But back numbers of a local newspaper . . .? And the *Fethering Observer* at that . . .? Graciously restrained, however, she did not share her opinion with the librarian. Just waited patiently while Di Thompson dealt with an elderly enquirer at the issue desk.

There was always a shelf of flyers for local events in the library. Yoga classes, cookery courses, a book group. Carole was not attracted to participate in any of them. She was not by nature a joiner. If the subject of such activities ever came up, she would say she was far too busy to get involved. Busy, busy, busy. The real reason was that she was afraid of exposing herself to the scrutiny of others.

There was a pile of flyers for a Pottery Open Day the following Wednesday. An invitation to visit the studio of Lauren Givens. Carole gave a mental snort (she was good at mental snorts). She had better things to do with her time than find out how ceramic toadstools were made.

Di Thompson, now free, helped her carry the blue-bound volumes to the desk that Carole had appropriated. The previous day, the librarian had explained the indexing that applied to the individual issues. The system had proved very inadequate, supplying far too little information. One or two major local topics, like the endless proposals for rerouting the bypass around Fedborough, had multiple references listed, but following lesser stories through was a matter of trial and error.

The two women knew each other well enough to exchange pleasantries. Carole had rejoined the library for those weekends when her two granddaughters, Lily and Chloe, came down to stay. She knew the fun the little girls could have there and, in a rather old-fashioned way, she preferred the idea of them reading books at High Tor than watching television. For her, words on a page would always be more worthy than images on a screen.

But Carole and Di Thompson would never have revived the other topic that had brought them together. Some years before it had happened – the murder of a visiting author in the library car park, for which Jude was at one stage the chief suspect . . . Well, that wasn't the kind of thing Carole Seddon would have continued to discuss with a librarian. When it came to polite conversation, she had her standards.

Her research that morning felt desultory. She had left the library the previous day, feeling that the back numbers of the *Fethering Observer* could yield a lot more information but, as she flicked through the pages, the law of diminishing returns kicked in. Most of the obvious stuff about Anita Garner's disappearance she had found the previous day. She was now shuffling through the newspapers' pages almost at random, hoping to chance on some new detail. And without marked success.

She recalled the other names which had been mentioned in the Crown and Anchor the previous evening. See if she could find any references to them. The Benyons' son Kent had been at school with Anita Garner. So had the extremely fortunate Glen Porter, who perhaps claimed to have had an affair with her . . . well, a 'thing' if not an affair . . . at least it had been asserted that he'd 'got inside her knickers'.

Then there was Roland Lasalle, builder's son, whose parents had put him through private school and university . . .

Carole did actually find a reference to Roland in a *Fethering Observer* from some twenty-five years ago. There was half a page of congratulatory flannel about the completion of his architectural training and his being offered a job at a very prestigious London practice 'working on many international projects'. He was referred to as 'son of well-known local builder and character Harry Lasalle, who is currently vice-commodore of Fethering

Yacht Club'. Harry claimed to be 'chuffed to bits' about his son's success. As was the boy's mother Veronica. 'Roly's always been a hard worker and I'm glad to see it's paid off for him'.

Until he took up his job in London, Roland Lasalle would be 'getting his hands dirty, helping out on various maintenance jobs that his father was working on in the Fethering area'.

There was a photograph of father and son. It didn't ring any bells for Carole, though. Had Jude been there, she would have recognized in the younger Harry Lasalle the greybeard she'd seen storming out of Footscrow House on the day Anita Garner's handbag was discovered.

A shadow came across the page Carole was reading. She looked up to see an almost emaciatedly thin man standing over her. His face was blotchy with age. A few tufts of hair rose proud of his cranium's tight skin. He wore what used to be called 'cavalry twill' trousers above thick sandals with socks and a pale blue zip-up 'windcheater' from another age.

'I'm so sorry to interrupt you,' he said, 'but it is rarely that a writer witnesses someone reading his own work. Of course, it might be more prestigious if the work being read were in the form of a literary novel published by Faber & Faber or Jonathan Cape, rather than in the pages of the *Fethering Observer*, but it is still a rare honour, of which I am appropriately aware.'

Carole was so surprised by this long speech that it was one of those rare moments when she could think of nothing to say. A smile crinkled across the old man's face as he continued, 'I'm sorry. I should have introduced myself. Though, in fact, I do conveniently have a visual aid for just such a purpose.'

He pointed down to the by-line of the piece about Roland Lasalle that Carole was reading. '"Malk Penberthy",' he read out. 'At your service. And for many years at the service of the *Fethering Observer* and its diminishing number of readers. A career of dedicated journalism which, while it may not have scaled the heights of front-page terrorist atrocities in the national dailies, did keep the good burghers of Fethering apprised of new brides' honeymoon plans, thefts of underwear from washing lines, and the all-important results of local dog shows. May I ask whom I have the honour of addressing?'

'My name is Carole Seddon.'

'Enchanted to meet you. And would I be imposing on your goodwill were I to ask you what prompts your avid perusal of that fine, though underestimated, organ, the *Fethering Observer*?'

She could see no point in dissembling. 'I am trying to find out more about the disappearance of Anita Garner.'

'Ah. Some time ago – thirty years we're talking now – but still one of the great Fethering mysteries. One of the great *unsolved* Fethering mysteries, I should say.'

'And one that you covered in your professional capacity?' She found that, inadvertently, she was dropping into his rather old-fashioned mandarin style of speech.

'Oh yes, I did. Many was the unprovable theory, false lead and wild rumour I pursued in that quest.'

Carole caught a look from Di Thompson. Though the old cartoon image of library staff constantly saying 'Ssh' no longer obtained, the expression did suggest that her domain was not the ideal setting for extended dialogue.

'I wonder, Malk,' said Carole, 'would you have time to join me for a cup of coffee?'

The two of them were united in regret at the closing, some years previously, of Polly's Cake Shop on the Fethering Parade. Malk was no longer working at the time of the murder that took place there, but he still knew everything about it. His interest in all things Fethering, nurtured throughout his life, was not going to be diminished by something as trivial as retirement.

They agreed too that the Starbucks which had replaced Polly's as the only dedicated coffee shop in the village was a poor substitute. Though the Crown and Anchor had all the latest Italian machines to produce the full gamut of Americanos, macchiatos, flat whites and so on, they also agreed that it didn't feel right going to a pub just for a coffee. And what passed under the name of coffee at the Seaview Café was only instant.

They were both surprised that, as the remorseless tread of coffee culture took over the whole country, no one had taken the initiative to open a new franchise-free individual venue in Fethering. Such businesses seemed to be springing up all along the South Coast. Maybe there was an entrepreneurial opportunity for someone there?

Carole couldn't believe her good fortune in having found – or it might be more accurate to say 'stumbled upon' – Malk Penberthy. She couldn't wait to tell Jude about her discovery. Unlike Barney Poulton, that incomer whose vaunted omniscience was now totally discredited, the retired journalist really could claim to be 'the eyes and ears of the village'.

And his memory was startlingly good. The *Fethering Observer* always came out on a Thursday and Malk could be specific about not only each article he wrote on the Anita Garner mystery but also the date on which it was published. He remembered the name of every person he'd interviewed in connection with the disappearance and had almost total recall of what they had said. Carole could not have found a more perfect and willing witness.

And Malk Penberthy responded to her interest. Perhaps retirement had made him feel marginalized from the world of news-gathering and he was just delighted to have his expertise valued once again. He visibly enjoyed engaging in speculation with her.

But, of course, the one vital question to which he could not provide an answer was: what had happened to Anita Garner?

Meticulously, he went through the various possibilities which had been discussed at the time and since. Some of these conjectures Carole had heard before, but she made notes of the ones she hadn't. Anita's parents, Malk said, had been little help, no less confused than anyone else. The mother had been the more approachable. Mr Garner, a staunchly old-fashioned Catholic, had clearly been obsessed by his daughter and objected strongly to any suggestions of impropriety in her behaviour. Which had made interviewing him a frustrating process.

'If he had discovered that she had been up to something he would have disapproved of,' asked Carole eagerly, 'how do you think he would have reacted?'

Malk Penberthy smiled and shook his head. 'Oh, Carole, Carole, we've all been there in our conjectures. I considered that scenario. Worshipped daughter admits to having had sex before marriage – or something worse – and obsessed father, in a fit of righteous anger, destroys the malefactor to keep her image unsullied. The Fethering version of an "honour killing". Is that the direction in which your thoughts might have been tending?'

'Maybe,' Carole admitted diffidently.

'A nice dramatic solution, I agree, that would work well as the climax of some shoddy television drama. But not one that can withstand scrutiny. At the time of his daughter's disappearance, Mr Garner had been in hospital in Clincham, being treated for prostate cancer. He'd been there two weeks and didn't come home until a couple of days after the last sighting of Anita.'

'Ah.'

'Yes, I'm sorry. Logic and reality have a distressing capacity for squashing our most intriguing hypotheses.'

'And where was this "last sighting"?'

'Footscrow House. Then a care home. Some of the staff saw her in the evening. Next morning, no sign of her. And there hasn't been from that day to this.'

'Hm.' Carole nodded thoughtfully. 'So, you didn't get any impression of hidden rifts within the Garner family?'

'Sadly, no.' Malk related how father and mother had been happy to have their grown-up daughter living with them and Anita herself had seemed equally contented with the arrangement. Her parents had felt confident she would leave home eventually to get married, 'but the right man hasn't come along yet'.

Yes, she had had boyfriends, but none of them seemed to last that long. Anita might be a little cast down at the end of each relationship; not for long, though. She was resilient and bounced back quickly. It was Mrs Garner's view that her daughter had 'never been properly in love'. And back then she'd reckoned 'there was time enough for that'.

No, Anita had never got depressed. She 'had her head screwed on all right'. She wasn't the sort to 'get all teary' over a man. She had more sense.

And yes, Mrs Garner was sure there had been men at work who'd come on to her from time to time. For an attractive young woman, that went with the territory. But Anita had been quite capable of telling any man who tried it on 'to keep his hands to himself'. And she'd never complained to her mother about suffering 'unwanted advances'.

Malk Penberthy, like the conscientious reporter he was, had followed up at a good few of Anita Garner's places of work, the shops, pubs and restaurants where she had been employed. And he had found the girl to have been well-liked in all of them. She could take a joke and had joined in the usual badinage of workplace flirtation. She had even on occasion gone out with colleagues, but nothing serious seemed to have developed with any of them.

'What about,' asked Carole, 'relationships in her final job? At Footscrow House when it was a care home?'

'Nothing substantiated there.'

She was quick to pounce on the words. '"Nothing substantiated"? Are you suggesting there were rumours?'

For the first time, Malk Penberthy looked uncomfortable. 'Oh, there are always rumours around any workplace. Bosses coming on to workers, that kind of thing. Once again, goes with the territory. And it was worse back then, before all this "Me Too" movement started. Those were the days when a licence to let one's hands wander was reckoned to be one of the perks of management. No young girl would have had the nerve to report anything. But, when I was investigating it, I got no proof that anything of the kind happened at the care home.'

Carole's instinct to ask supplementary questions was curbed by the ex-journalist continuing quickly, 'There was only one work relationship of Anita's I found out about which might have been more significant.'

And he related how, in the course of her peripatetic employment history, Anita Garner had worked behind the bar at the Cat and Fiddle, a riverside pub on the Fether, just on the edge of the South Downs. Malk had talked to its rather over-the-top landlady, Shona Nuttall, and been told that Anita had taken quite a shine to a young Spanish barman called Pablo. It was Shona's view that, even though they were both Catholics, something quite steamy had been going on there.

Then Pablo had suddenly been called back home by news of his mother's serious illness. His family lived in Cádiz. But Shona was convinced the young couple had stayed in touch.

'And what is interesting,' he warmed to his task, 'is that Anita had never expressed any interest in travelling abroad, but – and I got this from her mother – only weeks before she disappeared, she had applied for a passport. Which arrived at the house. Her mother saw the envelope.

'From which one might extrapolate that her daughter had got the passport simply so that she could join her lover in Spain.'

'Did the police investigate that possibility?'

A rueful grin from Malk Penberthy. 'Half-heartedly, if at all.'

'Hm.' Carole removed her rimless glasses and polished them thoughtfully.

'Anyway, for want of something better,' said Malk Penberthy, spreading his hands wide in a gesture of helplessness, 'that's the nearest I got to an explanation for Anita Garner's disappearance.'

'Well, I'm sorry to put a damper on your theory,' Carole apologized, 'but I'm afraid it won't hold up.'

'Why not?'

'Because, to travel to Spain, Anita Garner would have needed her passport.'

'And, if you were listening, Carole, I did just say that she had recently been issued with one.'

'But she didn't use it to go to Spain.'

'How do you know that?'

And she explained to Malk about the discovery of the handbag. And its contents.

He looked really crestfallen. Not because his theory had been ruled out, but because he had been excluded from the sources of information. If Malk Penberthy had still been a working journalist, he would have found out from Fethering Police about the find at Footscrow House. Now he was just another curious member of the public, with no special access to anything.

They had both finished their coffees and it seemed Malk had given as much relevant information as he could. He suddenly looked very tired, and Carole found herself wondering how old he actually was.

'I do hope you wouldn't mind if I were to contact you to pick your brains further . . .?' she asked, again surprised at how easily she slipped into his formal style of speaking.

'Nothing would give me greater pleasure,' he said. And then, going positively Jane Austen, 'I should like it of all things.'

'Well, let's exchange phone numbers.'

'An excellent idea, Carole. I'm afraid mine is a landline . . . though why I should apologize for that, I'm not quite sure.

However, in these days of smartphones and online this and online that, I feel obliged to do so. I do possess some primitive form of mobile phone, but I'm afraid I never got on with it. We didn't bond. The outdated notion that the sole purpose of a telephone is to make telephone calls was so much a part of my professional life that it is still engrained in my soul. *Mea culpa*. It is fortunate perhaps that I had to retire from journalism when I did. I enjoyed the daily to-and-fro of searching people out and talking to them. Today's generation of journalists do most of their work without taking their eyes off the screen on their office desks.'

Carole found herself warming increasingly to him. Though she could not now live without her laptop, and was using her smartphone more, his attitude to technology struck a chord deep within her.

Malk Penberthy was her sort of man.

Jude picked up the phone. It was Pete.

'Just wanted to check – still all right for me to start work at your place on Monday?'

'No problem at all. Be good to see you.'

That was true. It was always good to see Pete. But a little bit of Jude's satisfaction came from the thought that he might be able to tell her more about the history of Footscrow House. Which could of course be helpful in solving the mystery of Anita Garner's disappearance, now becoming something of an obsession.

'So, you'll be there, will you? I won't need a key?'

'No, I'll be here.' A moment of caution. 'What time do you start?'

'Eight.'

'Eight?' She hadn't got any clients booked in for the Monday morning. The thought of not being able to sleep in held little appeal. 'I'll give you a key. Shall I drop it in at Footscrow House?'

'No, I'm on another job now, up at Fedborough. Back at Fiasco House after I finish with you. Tell you what . . . if you drop in to the Fethering Yacht Club round twelve on Saturday . . .'

'Tomorrow?'

'Tomorrow as ever is. And at the yacht club you can give me a key . . . and I can buy you a drink.'

'What a nice idea,' said Jude.

FIVE

That evening the two women met at High Tor. Usually, if it was coffee, they sat in the kitchen. But Jude had brought a nice cold bottle of New Zealand Sauvignon Blanc and, for some complex reason related to her middle-class upbringing, Carole insisted they should drink it in the sitting room.

Jude was easy with this. Unlike her neighbour, she was easy with everything that didn't matter. She didn't, in the words of a self-help book she really deeply disliked, 'sweat the small stuff'. (Like almost all self-help books, in her view, almost every sentence in it was just another way of saying the message in the title.)

So, they sat in the sitting room, which at High Tor was exclusively a room for *sitting* in. Not a room for lounging or flopping in, like the one at Woodside Cottage.

Both women had major news to impart, but Carole insisted they shouldn't start talking about 'the case' until they were both seated in the sitting room's rather hard armchairs with a glass of Sauvignon Blanc in their hands.

Then, she managed to get in her bombshell first. 'I've met this wonderful man!' she said.

'Well, congratulations!' Jude responded. 'I kept telling you that, if you waited long enough, the right one would come along.'

Carole's pale cheeks coloured and, behind their rimless glasses, her eyelashes fluttered with annoyance. 'No, not that kind of "wonderful man"! Really, Jude, you do, on occasion, have something of a one-track mind. The man I am referring to is wonderful because he is a potential source of information.'

'Oh,' said Jude, appropriately subdued but with the slightest bubble of laughter in her voice.

Carole described her encounter with Malk Penberthy, concluding, 'And he really does know everything that's happened in Fethering for the past fifty years. He could be terribly useful to us if we have another murder investigation after this one.'

Jude looked at her neighbour quizzically. 'Are you saying the Anita Garner case is a murder investigation, Carole?'

'Well, of course it is! Why else would we be getting so interested in it?'

Jude reflected for a moment before saying, 'You could be right.'

'Of course I'm right! What else do you think happened to the poor girl?'

'That's a question to which nobody has found the answer for the past thirty years.'

'Well, maybe. But we weren't on the case then. We've only just started investigating.'

Jude grinned. Though Carole could sometimes be almost crippled by self-doubt, it was wonderful to see her in an up mood, with the bit between her teeth.

'Anyway, the main question,' Carole galloped on, 'is who knew about her relationship with Pablo? And whose nose did it put out of joint?'

'Sorry, just a minute. Pablo? Who's Pablo?'

'Oh, didn't I tell you?'

'No.'

Carole recounted what Malk had said about what was possibly Anita Garner's most serious relationship.

'And what was his source for that information?'

'Someone we've met, Jude.'

'Who?'

'Shona Nuttall.'

'Oh yes, I remember her. Used to be landlady of that ghastly pub on the Fether. The Cat and Fiddle. We met her when we were investigating the poisoning at the Crown and Anchor.'

'That's right.'

'Is she still around?'

'Don't know. Malk talked to her around the time of the disappearance, so we're talking thirty years ago. It was at the Cat and Fiddle, though, that Anita and Pablo met.'

'Ah. And did Anita say to anyone that she was planning to join this Pablo in Spain?'

'Not in so many words, no.'

'What does that mean?'

'It means she didn't say anything to anyone,' said Carole, a little shamefacedly.

'Incidentally . . .' Jude suddenly produced a scrap of paper from her pocket. 'I know when she applied for the passport.'

'How?'

'I wrote down the details before I gave the handbag to the police.' She pointed. 'There's the date of issue. Does that tally with the date of her disappearance?'

Carole nodded. 'Issued exactly three weeks before. So, it definitely looks as if she was planning some kind of trip abroad.'

'All right . . .' Jude sighed. 'Let's follow this theory a little way. Anita, who has never before expressed any interest in leaving the UK, suddenly applies for a passport, with a view to joining lover boy in Cádiz. Her departure is imminent, which is why she has her shiny new passport in her handbag.'

'But then someone' – Carole picked up the thread – 'took that handbag and shut it away behind a panel in Footscrow House for thirty years. Why would they want to do that?'

'More importantly,' asked Jude, 'who would want to do that?'

It was a long time since Jude had been to Fethering Yacht Club but the interior was unchanged. The main feature of the bar was a sea-facing window that filled an entire wall. It muffled the sound of metal cables clacking against masts in the winter wind. And the eternal swishing of the sea. And it enabled the owners to look out at their boats, lined up on the hardstanding between clubhouse and beach.

After dark, the window picked up reflections of the rows of bottles behind the bar opposite. By day, it opened on to the restless vista of the English Channel, rendered more turbulent by the waters of the Fether, which ran along the side wall of the yacht club. The river was tidal until way beyond Fedborough on the edge of the South Downs, which meant that twice a day the phenomenon would be seen of water flowing upstream. (This set up a complex system of currents where the Fether met the sea, a hazard which had caused a good few fatalities over the years. The bodies of those unfortunates who fell in the river tended, within a few days, to wash up on the beach. They had been known for many years as 'Fethering Floaters'.)

The fascination exerted by the sea was such that, though there were stools by the bar, the most popular seats were lined up in front of the drinks shelf that ran along the big window. There, members could while away the hours, nursing a pint, watching the shifting seascape and thinking whatever thoughts they wished to think. That Saturday, the vista which opened out to them was icy, steel-grey and fretful.

Jude had been surprised when Pete had said he was a member of Fethering Yacht Club. One of her previous contacts there, a former vice-commodore called Denis Woodville, now long dead, had been insistent on the club's exclusivity and unwillingness to admit 'riff-raff'. And, though many of the locals would strenuously deny the accusation, there were very rigid social divisions in Fethering. Even in the twenty-first century, there was still a distinction between people in the professions and those in trade. How would the average decorator get through the arcane membership selection process for the yacht club?

The question just made Jude more aware of how different Pete was from 'the average decorator'. As was often repeated round Fethering, nobody had a bad word to say about Pete. His enthusiasm for sailing and his skill at the sport were unquestioned. Over the years, he had won most of the club's available trophies. And maybe he had been admitted to membership at a time of less social snobbery.

When Jude entered the bar, Pete was sitting at the counter with a pint in front of him, talking to a couple, one of whom she recognized. It was Lauren Givens, the woman she'd encountered earlier in the week on Fethering Beach. And the way they sat together suggested that the man beside her was her husband, the rich one who reputedly spent his weeks working at marketing in London while his wife crafted ceramic toadstools in Fethering.

Jude saw that, as ever, there were other members by the window, contemplating the unending sequence of the tides, the ever-changing image of the English Channel.

Pete, who'd clearly been on the lookout, rose from his stool to greet her. 'Glad you could make it, love. What can I get you?'

'Sauvignon Blanc'd be good. New Zealand if they've got it.'

'Sure they have. Don't know if you know Fred and Lauren Givens . . .?'

Jude grinned at the woman, 'We've sort of met, haven't we?'

Lauren nodded a little awkwardly. While Pete attracted the barmaid's attention, her husband rose and held out a hand to Jude. Fred Givens was a tall man with expertly groomed grey hair. He wore leisurewear so immaculate that it contrived to look like formalwear.

'Jude – my husband Fred.'

'Nice to meet you.'

'Jude, the pleasure's all mine.' His manner was as smooth as his appearance. 'And I hope to see a lot more of you.'

'Oh?' said Jude, slightly puzzled.

'The fact is, Jude, that I'm hoping to get to know a lot more Fethering residents a lot better. I was just talking to Pete about it.'

'About what?' She gratefully took the drink that Pete held out for her.

It was the decorator who answered her question. 'Fred was telling me about the benefits of "working from home". During all that lockdown caper he had no choice, no office to go to. And now he's got a taste for it.'

'You can say that again,' Fred Givens enthused. 'Enlightenment came upon me as I sat in my delightful house in De Vere Road. Why should I have this divided life? Weekdays in London, weekends in Fethering . . . doesn't make sense. So, during the lockdown, I got into a very nice routine, turned one of the spare bedrooms into a home office, set up all the technology I need there. Marketing these days is mostly a matter of dealing with figures and you don't need an office to do that – you just need a laptop. So, now I can move around again, if I've got meetings, I go up to London . . . what, one day, two days a week? And the rest of the time I can benefit from the delights of Fethering. Works a treat. I've got my little workstation upstairs, Lauren potters around with her pottery downstairs – it's the perfect work/life balance.'

The expression on his wife's face suggested that she didn't fully share his enthusiasm for the situation. And, also, that she'd heard the witticism 'potters around with her pottery' many times before. 'Perfect for you, maybe, Fred,' she said.

The level of venom in Lauren's words made Jude think a

change of subject might avert a marital row. So, in classic English style, she fell back on the weather. 'God, the heavens opened that day when I saw you on the beach, didn't they, Lauren?'

'What? When?' A look of confusion.

'Thursday. We met just by the beach huts.'

'Oh yes, of course.'

'I walked back slowly, getting soaked to the bone. And you ran off home, like a murderer leaving the scene of the crime.'

Lauren still looked confused. Jude chuckled. 'What'd you been doing that you shouldn't have been, Lauren?'

But there was no response. This time, Pete came to the conversational rescue. 'Of course, I was just pointing out to Fred that working from home is all right for some. If I tried it, soon I wouldn't be able to move for the layers of paint and wallpaper.'

Fred Givens enjoyed the joke. 'Good one, Pete,' he said with just a hint of condescension. Jude got the impression that, in his attitude to the decorator, he was very definitely demonstrating his 'common touch'.

Maybe Pete was aware of the slight because he said, 'Need to sort out stuff with Jude,' and steered her away from the couple at the bar. As he did so, he caught the eye of someone he recognized who'd arrived only a few minutes earlier. A tall man with foppishly long grey hair.

'Hello, Glen,' said Pete.

Jude couldn't believe her luck. Carole had fallen on her feet meeting Malk Penberthy and now she was being offered an equivalent moment of serendipity. There couldn't be that many people in a village like Fethering called Glen. There was a strong chance this must be the financially fortunate Glen Porter, the man who had been at school with Anita Garner and who claimed to have been inside her knickers.

'Oh, hi, Pete,' came the reply, as the new arrival scanned the room, starting with the sea-gazers by the window and ending with the groups at the bar. Jude waited to be introduced.

But at that moment, Glen Porter clapped his hand on the back pocket of his trousers, said, 'Oh damn, I've left my phone in the car', and departed the bar.

Almost exactly in the way that Lauren Givens had behaved on Fethering Beach. A more paranoid person than Jude might have begun to take it personally. What was it that made people invent elaborate excuses to avoid meeting her? Well, actually not that elaborate. Claiming to have forgotten one's mobile must be about the most obvious excuse there is these days. Still, not much of a booster for her self-esteem.

She sat with Pete, looking out of the window. Low tide and the sea was almost out of sight. Beyond the stout seawalls that contained the outflow of the River Fether, acres of sand and another line of dark shingle were exposed.

'Oh, while I think . . .' said Jude, handing across a spare key.

'Thanks.' Pete pocketed it. Had he been a man of burglarious tendencies, the decorator could have stripped the contents of almost every house in Fethering. Over the years, he'd had so many keys and plenty of time to get them copied. But the thought would not have entered his head. (And, anyway, a light-fingered workman would never be employed again in a community like Fethering.)

'Do just come and go as you please,' Jude went on. 'You said you reckoned you'd be finished within the week . . .?'

'Shouldn't even take that long.' Pete grinned. 'Depending, of course, on how many "Oh-while-you're-heres" we get.'

'I'll try to keep them to a minimum.'

'Everyone says that.'

'We'll see. Anyway, you can spread yourself, no need to tidy up at the end of the day. I won't be using the room. No clients booked in for the whole week. A few I may visit in their homes. But I'll be safe to take bookings again for Monday week, will I?'

'Sure.'

'Won't still be a smell of paint? Some clients might find that off-putting.'

'It'll have the weekend to clear. So long as you keep the room well ventilated, should be all right.'

'Fine. I'll see the windows are open.'

Pete looked at her with his toothy grin. 'Anything else you want me to do while I'm there?'

'What do you mean? Decorating?'

'No. Other stuff. Over the years I've been asked to take on a lot of . . . extra responsibilities. Before so many people had answering machines and then mobile phones, I was sometimes like a blooming social secretary when I was in their houses. Unpaid babysitter, and all, at times. "I'm just nipping out to the shops. He'll be asleep for at least an hour, so I'll easily be back before he wakes." And then, of course, her closing the front door is the little one's cue to wake up bawling with a dirty nappy.'

'That's one problem you won't have at Woodside Cottage,' said Jude.

'No, but I'm also up for paying the window-cleaner, letting in the man to mend the Aga, cat-sitting, dog-walking, watering plants . . . you name it, I've done it. These days, mind you, it's mostly taking in deliveries from Amazon.'

'You won't have that problem either. I don't believe in Amazon.'

'Good for you. All I'm saying, Jude, is: anything like that you need doing, fine by me.'

'Thank you. I'll let you know if anything's likely to come up.'
'No probs.'

There was a silence. Jude looked out at the sea. Pete caught the eye of someone sitting on his own at the far end of the window and nodded acknowledgement. Jude looked across and recognized the heavily built grey-bearded man she'd seen hurrying out of Footscrow House the day they'd found the handbag. In profile, she could see that his lower jaw jutted out more than the upper, so that his bite did not align. Maybe that was why he had grown the beard.

She hoped Pete would go across and introduce her, but the decorator had other priorities.

'It seems,' he said, 'that all the old gossip about Anita Garner's starting up again.'

'Yes, I've heard a bit,' agreed Jude, sounding as casual as she could. She didn't want to acknowledge that she and Carole might have been partly responsible for that 'starting up'. 'You found out anything more?'

The decorator looked momentarily shifty, then leaned close and whispered to her, 'I found out exactly when that handbag was left there, you know, when that decorating job was done.'

'Really?'

'Footscrow House was still a care home then, but the owner had decided things weren't working out. It was his first go at running one. And his last. He was always trying to expand the business into different areas, and reckoned there was easy money to be made in care homes. But he bit off more than he could chew there – and no mistake.' The decorator chuckled softly, still unwilling to be overheard.

'Who are we talking about, Pete?'

'Oh, I'm sorry.' Now in a whisper, 'Harry Lasalle. Harry Lasalle and his wife Veronica ran Fiasco House when it was a care home.' He nodded towards the grey-bearded man. 'That's him over there.'

This time, again catching the older man's eye, Pete stood up and said, to Jude's great satisfaction, 'Come and meet him.'

Introductions completed, Pete asked, 'How're you doing?'

'Can't complain.' Harry Lasalle laughed bitterly. 'Not that that stops me from complaining all the bloody time.'

Pete pointed to the empty tumbler on the shelf. 'Get you another? What are you on?'

'Whisky. It's that bad.'

'Any particular one?'

'Teacher's'd be great.'

'Coming up. And you'll have another of them Cab Sauves, Jude?'

'It really should be my turn.'

'Nonsense. Only members allowed to buy drinks in Fethering Yacht Club.'

Whether that was true or not, Jude accepted gracefully. She turned to Harry Lasalle, whose face had a mournful, even haunted, look. 'Actually, I saw you earlier in the week.'

'Oh?' He didn't sound that interested.

'You were coming out of Footscrow House.'

'Could have been.'

'I was there to meet up with Pete.'

'Right.' He didn't give the impression of finding that any more interesting.

'And did you hear – we found Anita Garner's handbag in there.'

He was clearly shaken, but his only response was, 'That's a name I haven't heard for a while.' And he moved quickly on. 'Yes, we're doing some work down at Footscrow. Well, I say "we", like I was still involved. In fact, my son's in charge now. It's his project, not Lasalle Build and Design.'

There was a lot of bitterness in his voice. 'Still, you shouldn't expect to get gratitude from your kids these days. Oh no. You look after them, you subsidize them, you make excuses for them, you cover up for them – and do you get a word of thanks? Do you hell? I think there comes a time when parents should call in the debts their kids have built up. Do you have children?'

'No.'

'Then you're bloody lucky. You won't get one of your kids acing you out of a juicy work contract. Not, of course, that I can do much actual work these days, but my bloody son could have brought me in on a consultancy basis. It's not like I don't know the business inside out.'

'You say you can't do much actual work . . .?'

'Back problems.'

'I'm sorry to hear that.' Maybe she could genuinely help him, using her healing skills. But the thought wasn't purely altruistic. She also saw the opportunity to find out more about his dealings with the missing woman. 'If you want someone to check out your back, I'm actually a qualified—'

'I don't want anything, thank you! Been to the quack, they can't do anything. What's wrong with my back is down to a lifetime of heavy lifting. Can't be cured.'

'Well, if you would like me to—'

She was interrupted by the return of Pete with the drinks. He'd got another pint for himself. They clinked and cheersed.

Pete looked down at the boats drawn up in symmetrical formation on the hardstanding. '*Harry's Dream* still afloat, is she?'

'Oh yes,' said the builder grimly. 'More than can be said for her owner.'

'Which one is she?' asked Jude, pleased to get the pronoun right.

Harry pointed down to a tarpaulin-covered boat on a trailer below. 'Cornish Shrimper 19 she is. Well, she is now. Hardly was when I bought her. Just a hull then. Damage to the fibreglass shell, interior wood rotting. I replaced virtually every stick of timber in her.'

'Real labour of love, wasn't it, Harry?'

'You can say that again, Pete. And I built berths in there, equipped a galley with a gas cooker and what-have-you. Interior heating, ship's toilet, all mod cons. Took me years.'

Harry Lasalle looked more cheerful than he had since their conversation started. 'You know, I done all kinds of major building projects along the South Coast – big houses, conversions, civic developments . . . you name it. And still, the thing I'm proudest of is that boat down there.'

'That's why you called it *Harry's Dream* – right?'

'Yup, Pete, that's right.' Gloom suddenly reasserted itself. 'Mind you, I don't know how much longer I'm going to keep her.'

'You thinking of getting rid of *Harry's Dream*?' The decorator sounded shocked. 'You can't be serious.'

The old man grimaced. 'Well, what's the use of a boat if you don't take it on the water?'

'You said she was fine. There's nothing wrong with her, is there?'

'Nothing wrong with *her*, no. Get on to me and that's another matter.'

'Don't do yourself down, Harry.'

'It's true, Pete. I used to be able to sail her on my own, no problem. Cross-Channel trips, booze cruises, you name it. Then sometimes the wife crewed for me, but the arthritis got into her legs and she can't do it no more. And way back, my boy'd come out with me, but he's got other fish to fry now. So, there's no way I can actually sail her, not with my back.'

'I'd be happy to crew for you, Harry.'

'I know you would, Pete, and I appreciate the offer. But fact is, helming in anything but the calmest of conditions is painful, back gives me so much gyp. So that means . . . what? I can take the boat out, using the motor, but that's not what I built her for. *Harry's Dream*'s a sailing boat, a yacht, we're here in a yacht club. No, I think I'll sell her.'

'Don't make any hasty decisions,' said Pete.

'Won't be hasty. I've been thinking about it for years.'

'Well, think a bit longer. You still like going fishing from her, don't you?'

'I don't know,' came the glum reply. 'I'm getting bored with that, and all. Getting bored with everything.'

'Don't sell her, Harry.'

'Maybe I won't. Maybe I'll take her out for one last trip . . . with the bloody motor. See if I can get interested in fishing again. Huh. We'll see.' Harry Lasalle looked at his watch. 'Time I was off. Thanks for the drink, Pete. And nice to meet you . . .'

Purely automatic politeness. He hadn't taken in her name.

'Jude.'

'That's right. Cheerio.' He winced as he rose from his stool and moved a little unsteadily towards the door. Jude wondered whether it was back pain that compromised his movement or the number of double Teacher's he'd downed. The one Pete had bought him hadn't lasted long.

On his way to the exit, the old builder was stopped by Lauren Givens, who had left her bar stool to head him off. Jude couldn't hear what they were saying, but the woman seemed to be asking Harry for something. Whatever it was, he didn't grant what she wanted. Harry Lasalle tottered on out of the bar. Lauren returned, with a disgruntled expression, to join her husband.

Pete took a thoughtful swallow of beer. 'Tough for him, poor old Harry. It'll be tough for me when I get to that point.'

'What do you mean?'

'Manual labour, Jude. It catches up with you, if you've spent your entire life working in a trade where you're just reliant on your body.'

'But you're not just reliant on your body, Pete. Don't do yourself down. Some of your work I've seen definitely qualifies as art.'

He chuckled. 'Kind of you to say so. And I dare say, over the years, Harry has developed a kind of artistic sense over all the building projects he's done. But the fact remains that, for both of us, to do our job, we need to be fit. Our bodies have got to work. And, once bits of the old body stop working . . . well, you can't go on. I can't see Harry sitting behind a desk in the office, doing the admin. He'd be bored to tears in no time. Anyway, Veronica's always done that stuff.

'So, poor bugger's going to have to throw in the towel soon and retire. Then what does he do?'

'Doesn't he have any hobbies?'

'Always obsessed by his work, Harry was. Only time he could forget about it was when he was out sailing on *Harry's Dream*. And, like you just heard, he can't do that any more. Again, the old body's let him down.'

'Hm.' Jude took a thoughtful sip of Sauvignon Blanc. 'And you said it'll be the same for you, Pete.'

'Well, it will. Decorators get lots of neck problems, shoulders and knees at risk too. I'm not there yet, thank God, but there's going to come a time when I can't shift wardrobes to paint behind them and I can't spend the whole day up a ladder. Yes, it'll come to me too.'

'Let's hope you're still able to sail.' She looked out of the window. 'Which one's yours?'

The decorator pointed proudly to a sailing boat which, to Jude's inexperienced eye, looked just like all the others. But she still let out a suitably impressed 'Fabulous. And is it called "Pete's Dream"?'

'No. Nothing like that. *Gull's Wings.*'

'That's nice.'

'I like it. Wife and kids like it. So that's all fine.'

'Well, I hope you're able to sail . . . her' – oops, she'd almost said 'it' – 'long into your retirement. And if you can't . . . do you have any other hobbies to fall back on?'

'I do, actually.

'Oh. What?'

'I collect eighteenth-century glass.'

The answer was so unexpected that it prompted one of those rare moments when Jude was lost for words.

'So,' Pete went on, 'I'll be all right. There's enough to learn about eighteenth-century glass to keep me going for several lifetimes.' He sighed. 'But for someone like Harry . . . how's he going to fill the time?'

'How indeed?'

Pete grinned wryly. 'Hope it's not with the whisky.'

SIX

While her neighbour was at Fethering Yacht Club, Carole realized that there was some investigation she could do on her own. Though the two women collaborated well, there were times when she felt jealous of Jude's ease of manner and skill at drawing secrets out of people. Carole liked the feeling of exclusivity she got from doing a bit of private investigation and presenting Jude with the surprise of new information. That was why she enjoyed the element of secrecy inherent in her meetings with Malk Penberthy.

And it was a name he had mentioned that offered her a new line of enquiry. Shona Nuttall. Carole and Jude had first met her when she was landlady of the Cat and Fiddle, a Country & Western-themed pub on the River Fether, north of Fedborough. They had been investigating the death of Tadeusz Jankowski, brother of the Zosia who became Ted Crisp's bar manager.

Shona, who made her bar staff dress in gingham shirts and dungarees, had then been a tightly corseted, flamboyant figure, favouring shimmery tops, fake tan and too much jewellery. The wall behind the Cat and Fiddle bar was peppered with photographs of her embracing the pub's embarrassed regulars. She lived up almost too accurately to the stereotype of the big-hearted and big-bosomed landlady.

When Carole and Jude next met her, Shona had been considerably diminished, in personality if not in bulk. By then she'd been forced to sell the pub at far too low a price and lived behind closed curtains in a bungalow in Southwick, on the outskirts of Brighton. She shuffled round in jogging bottoms, appearing to spend her days smoking and drinking vodka.

Given these habits, and the number of years since they last met, Carole wondered whether Shona Nuttall was still in the land of the living. But she still had the woman's mobile number and it was worth trying.

To her surprise, it was quickly answered. 'Hallo?'

The voice had neither the brashness of Shona in full landlady mode, nor the whine of self-pity they'd encountered on their second meeting. It sounded certainly older, but alert and purposeful.

Carole identified herself. 'I don't know if you remember me.'

'I certainly do. You came to see me with your friend Jude, in connection with that Polish boy I employed at the Cat and Fiddle.'

Full marks for total recall, thought Carole. 'It's actually in connection with another of your employees at the pub that I'm calling.'

'Oh?'

'Anita Garner.'

'Oh, that poor, poor girl,' said Shona Nuttall. 'God rest her soul.'

It was still the same bungalow in Southwick, but its interior was totally transformed. Carole's recollection had been predominantly of velvet. Bottle-green velvet curtains, pink Dralon armchairs, cuddling photographs from the Cat and Fiddle in velvet-covered frames.

No sign of any of that. The curtains were now organic linen, the furniture plain wood, and there wasn't a photograph in sight. The effect was minimalist, almost Spartan.

Shona herself had become more minimalist too. In her corseted or uncorseted form, there had always been a lot of her, but since they last met, she must have shed at least four stone. Her body was now almost stringy. She wore a plain black dress and no jewellery.

Carole had not taken off her coat. There was no heating on in the bungalow. Shona did not offer her any refreshment. Instead, she sat down opposite and said, 'Anita Garner.'

'Yes.'

'Poor, deluded girl.'

'Why do you say that?'

'Because she was born and grew up as a Catholic.'

'And you regard Catholicism as a delusion?'

'Yes. Don't you?'

Carole didn't have much in the way of religion (except for writing 'C of E' on forms that asked the question). But she was of the view that it was a private matter. If people managed to have a faith, good for them. Lucky for them, perhaps. But she wouldn't get into arguments about the relative merits of individual faiths.

So, she answered Shona's question with an equivocating, 'It's not something I feel strongly about.'

'Oh, but you should feel strongly about it. Faith is too important not to have strong feelings about it.'

'Right,' said Carole cautiously.

'Have you invited Jesus into your life?' asked Shona.

'No. Not specifically.'

'Then I feel sorry for you, Carole.'

'Well, thank you for the kind thought. But I really wanted to talk about Anita Garner.'

'Catholics are not Christians,' Shona Nuttall announced.

'That's a point of view, certainly,' said Carole. 'But, again, it's not something I feel strongly about.'

Shona shook her head sadly. 'As I say, I feel sorry for you, Carole.'

'Thanks again. So, when Anita was on your staff at the Cat and Fiddle, I'm sure her Catholicism didn't affect her work, did it?'

'I don't know. Back then, I hadn't invited Jesus into my life.'

'Ah. Right.'

'I was entrapped in the toils of wickedness. I was encouraging evil, telling people to drink. I was a sinner, but now Jesus has cleansed me of my sins.'

'Oh. Good.'

'I used to drink myself, until Jesus told me not too. I was a bride of wickedness. Now I am a bride of Jesus.'

Carole couldn't think of an appropriate response to that, so she asked, 'Do you mind just thinking back to when Anita Garner worked for you at the Cat and Fiddle?'

'No. That's what you want to know about.'

'Yes.'

'It was an unhappy time of my life.'

'Oh, I'm sorry.'

'All of my life was unhappy, until I invited Jesus into it.'

'Obviously a sensible thing to do then.'

'Yes. The best thing I ever did. That is how I found happiness.

More than happiness. That is how I found bliss. When I invited Jesus into my life.'

Carole was beginning to get a little frustrated by the way her enquiries were constantly being deflected by Jesus. Raising her voice, she said, 'I also understand there was a young Spanish man called Pablo who worked for you at the Cat and Fiddle.'

'Yes. He was also a Catholic. Also deluded.'

'Maybe. But I've heard that Pablo and Anita . . . got close to each other.'

'They were in love,' said Shona. 'Though, of course, human love bears no comparison to the love of Jesus.'

'No. But,' Carole insisted, 'do you know how close to each other they were?'

'Do you mean: were they sleeping together?'

Relieved to get an answer that didn't involve Jesus, Carole said, 'Yes, that's exactly what I mean. Did you have staff accommodation at the Cat and Fiddle?'

'I did.'

'So, the young couple could have been sleeping together at—'

'No,' said Shona firmly. 'I wouldn't have allowed that. I did have moral standards, even before I invited Jesus into my life.'

'Oh, good.'

'Anyway, Anita never stayed overnight at the pub. Pablo did, but she always went home to her parents' house.'

'And then she stopped working for you and went to work at Footscrow House, when it was a care home. Is that right?'

'Yes.'

'And do you know if she and Pablo stayed in touch?'

'I'm pretty sure they did. They both seemed to be very keen.'

'And then he left the Cat and Fiddle?'

'Yes. Very suddenly. It was extremely inconvenient for me. Losing staff at short notice always is. But Pablo got a message that his mother was seriously ill. The family was from Cádiz and he rushed out there.'

'And did you ever hear from him again?'

'No.'

'And what about Anita? Did you see her after she left the pub?'

'I did, actually, yes. Bumped into her in Fedborough one day. About a week before she disappeared. I asked if she'd heard from Pablo.'

'And had she?'

'Yes. She said he'd rung her lots of times from Cádiz. His mother was still ill, so he was stuck out there. And then Anita told me what she was going to do.'

'Oh?'

'She said she was going out to Spain to see Pablo. She'd ordered a passport specially, so that she could make the trip out there.'

'Did you tell anyone what she'd told you?'

'Why should I? Who should I tell?'

'The police?'

'I've always kept clear of the police, thank you very much. They were never much help when I was running the Cat and Fiddle. Getting involved with them is just asking for trouble.'

'But, surely, knowing the fuss there was in the media about Anita Garner's disappearance . . . didn't you think what you knew was relevant?'

'Maybe I did, maybe I didn't. As I said, I was a bride of wickedness back then. It was before I had invited Jesus into my life.'

Before the Jesus litany started up again, Carole asked, 'So, you reckon Anita did go out to Cádiz?'

'Of course she did. It seems I'm the only person in the world who knows what happened to Anita Garner. She went out to Cádiz to join up with Pablo. She's probably still out there. He was Catholic too. Chances are they got married and started producing lots more deluded little Catholics. Anyway, I'm sure that's what happened. That's the solution to the mystery of the missing Anita Garner.

'But,' Shona went on, warming to her theme, 'Carole, I can tell you're unhappy. Don't despair, it's not too late to find happiness. Jesus will never turn you away. If you were to invite Jesus into your life, happiness would spread through you like . . .'

It had taken a while for Carole to extricate herself from the proselytizing Shona Nuttall. Clearly finding God had been a major event in the woman's life, but Carole did wonder whether God was equally pleased at being found.

As she drove the Renault thoughtfully back to Fethering, she considered the great flaw in the former landlady's theory.

Anita Garner may have intended to go out to Cádiz and be reunited with Pablo, but she never made the trip. Her unused passport remained in her handbag, immured in an alcove at Footscrow House.

'Is that Jude?'

She admitted it was. The voice at the other end of the phone was female, mature and aggressive.

Saturday evening. Jude had had a little zizz after she got back from Fethering Yacht Club, then cooked her main meal of the day, and was settling down for the evening to read a book that a friend had just published on the subject of *chakras*.

'I'm Veronica Lasalle,' said the woman, 'and I hear you've been stirring things up about Anita Garner.'

'What do you mean – "stirring things up"?'

'People around Fethering are talking about her again.'

'So? Why do you think I have anything to do with that?'

'You mentioned her to my husband at the yacht club.'

'Yes, all right, I did, but that was simply—'

'And that nosy neighbour of yours has been digging it all up again.'

'Carole is a—'

'Just stop it – right? There were a lot of lies told about Harry at the time. It was very hurtful to him. Had a bad effect on the business, too, for a while. But he hadn't done anything wrong. It was a long time ago and everyone had forgotten about it until you and your friend started digging.'

'All that happened was that Anita Garner's handbag was found and—'

'Listen, my husband's not in a good place at the moment. All this stuff coming up again is not going to help him. So, just lay off Harry – all right!'

And the line went dead. Jude got the impression that Veronica Lasalle was not a woman who was used to being crossed.

*   *   *

She had another unexpected call around eleven thirty on the Sunday morning. From Ted Crisp. Asking, rather shamefacedly, for the mobile number of Brandie Neville.

What the hell was going on there?

Then, early Sunday evening, Pete rang.

No, no problems about him starting work the following morning. But he thought she'd like to know; he'd just heard bad news from a friend at Fethering Yacht Club.

One of the members had noticed that morning that *Harry's Dream* was no longer on the hardstanding in front of the clubhouse. The club member had gone out in his own boat to an area where he knew Harry Lasalle had always enjoyed fishing. He'd found *Harry's Dream* anchored in the usual place.

But there was no sign of anyone about.

Having boarded the boat and opened the hatch to the cabin, the yachtsman had found Harry lying on the floor.

There was an empty whisky bottle beside him.

He was dead.

SEVEN

'Carbon monoxide poisoning,' said Pete.

'Really?'

'Yes, that's what killed him. After the alarm had been raised, the coastguard towed the boat back to the yacht club, then the police took over.'

'There's your coffee.' White with one sugar. Jude'd get used to that order over the week ahead. Pete's working life was fuelled by coffee. First day on a new job he'd bring his flask. Best to be prepared. With some clients he continued bringing the flask every day. He had reckoned Jude would have offered to make cups for him, but you could never be sure, working for a new client. However well you thought you knew them. People, Pete knew, were unpredictable.

As agreed, he'd arrived at Woodside Cottage at eight, let himself in and got started washing down the sitting-room walls. Jude had descended some forty-five minutes later, dressed in a voluminous, multi-coloured towelling robe. Though the central heating was on at full blast, the cold outside air somehow still infiltrated the house.

Her normal instinct, having made her cup of tea, would have been to take it back under the duvet, but that Monday morning she was much more interested in the news from Fethering Yacht Club.

'Where did you hear it from, Pete?'

'In the club, yesterday evening. No one was talking about anything else.'

'I bet they weren't. So, when did Harry take his boat out?'

'Early in the morning. Before it was light, they reckon.'

'Is that unusual, for people to take their boats out that early?'

'Unusual, yes. But it still happens quite a lot. Particularly with owners going on long trips, to France or wherever. A matter of getting the tides right, you see.'

'Of course. But, so far as you know, Harry wasn't planning a long trip?'

'No. They seemed to think he was just going out fishing. He did sometimes go out early for that. Harry used to be very keen on his fishing. Hasn't done so much of it recently, though. Probably because of his back problems. But there's an area about a mile out where he usually goes. Got some good catches out there, over the years. That's where *Harry's Dream* was found.'

'Hm.' Jude took a pensive sip of tea. 'And the carbon monoxide . . . where did that come from?'

'Heater in the cabin. He'd got that on full blast. If it wasn't properly ventilated . . . or there was a faulty valve . . . one or the other. You keep reading of these tragedies of kids in caravans and, you know . . .'

'Sure. When we saw Harry on Saturday, he said he'd done all the conversion work on *Harry's Dream* himself . . .'

'Yes. He was really proud of that boat.'

'Right.' Slowly, Jude pieced things together. 'So, an experienced builder like Harry Lasalle would have known all about the dangers from faulty heaters, wouldn't he?'

'Certainly would.'

'And he'd have known the safety precautions that had to be taken when installing them . . . and he'd have been particularly careful when he was doing the installation on his own boat . . .?'

'You betcha.'

'So, if there was a fault in the system, Harry would have known about it.'

'He'd have known all right,' said Pete.

'Could he actually have caused the fault?'

'You mean . . .?'

'He did sound pretty low when we talked to him on Saturday.'

Pete nodded thoughtfully. 'I hadn't thought of that possibility.'

'But he could have deliberately sabotaged the heater?'

'Certainly could. For anyone who'd been in the building trade as long as Harry, to set that up would not have been a problem.'

While Jude was dressing, she had a moment's doubt. Thinking of the phone call she'd had on the Saturday evening, was there any justice in Veronica Lasalle's accusations? Harry Lasalle's wife had berated Carole and Jude for 'stirring things up'. And now her husband was dead, possibly by his own hand.

Instinctively, Jude didn't feel any guilt, but she wondered whether she should. Whatever accusations had been made about Harry Lasalle at the time of Anita Garner's disappearance had been 'very hurtful'. They had even affected his business. Which must have meant the allegations were pretty serious.

But, from her brief acquaintance with the man, Jude hadn't got the impression of someone hypersensitive, who needed to be cotton-wooled. If he felt guilty enough to kill himself, then Jude reckoned he must have committed some offence against Anita Garner and was worried about the truth coming out, thirty years on.

This conclusion made her even more determined to find out the facts of what had happened. To which end, she went next door to High Tor and invited herself in for a cup of coffee. She had plenty to tell her neighbour.

Armed with the news of Veronica Lasalle's call to Jude and her husband's subsequent death, Carole announced that she was going to talk further to Malk Penberthy.

When the wind blew in directly off the sea, Fethering could be seriously cold. And that morning it was. But Jude had wrapped herself up in a long floral, faux-fur-lined coat she had bought for a fiver at a jumble sale. By way of fastenings, it had rope loops and toggles. She knew, if she didn't go out for a walk, she would never get her circulation going, and feel cold all day. Her other fallback heating option, lighting a fire in the sitting room, was off the menu because Pete was painting in there.

She pulled a burgundy woollen hat a long way down over her hair, shoved her hands in the coat's faux-fur-lined pockets and set off on her warming-up exercise. Reckoning the wind straight off the sea would be too chilling, she avoided the beach and walked along the residential streets north of Fethering Parade. As ever, she couldn't stop her mind from creating backstories to the lives lived behind all those respectable front windows.

But these speculations could not entirely shut out of her mind thoughts of Harry Lasalle and Anita Garner.

She heard her mobile ring. Damn, it was in the pocket of her fleece, under the coat.

By the time she had negotiated the toggles and the faux-fur, the caller had resorted to leaving a message.

Brandie. Jude called her back. 'How're you doing, love?'

'Fine. Just wanted to ask you something.'

'Ask away.'

'About Ted Crisp.'

'Oh?'

'What kind of person is he, Jude?'

'What kind of person? Well, he's . . . er . . .'

'I think he has a good soul.'

'Yes. Yes, Brandie. Nothing wrong with his soul.'

'You said that as if there are other parts of his personality where things aren't so healthy.'

'Did I? I didn't mean to. No, Ted's . . . well, he's . . . He's very kind. He's been a good friend to me over the years. He's . . . um . . . well, he's probably not exactly at the sharp end of the political-correctness spectrum. And his sense of humour is . . . Well, he used to be a stand-up comic but it didn't really work out for him. Even Ted himself would admit that his jokes are lousy. Sorry, Brandie, why are you asking me this?'

'Because I'm going to have lunch with him today.'

'Oh. Very nice. Where? At the Crown and Anchor?'

'No, at a vegan restaurant in Brighton.'

Vegan? Ted Crisp? What the hell was going on?

Inevitably, it was Starbucks again. Malk Penberthy looked less relaxed than he had at their previous meeting there.

'You've heard, presumably, about Harry Lasalle?' Carole began in a businesslike way, once they were at a table with their coffees.

'Yes. I may not still have the range of information conduits I once had, but that news did filter through the Fethering bush telegraph.'

'My neighbour Jude met him for the first time on Saturday. He was very down, she said. The consensus seems to be that he committed suicide.'

He smiled. 'Is there anywhere on God's earth where a consensus can build up more quickly than in Fethering? As to the verdict of suicide, I wouldn't be qualified to comment on that. One thing my journalistic training did teach me is that one should never announce conclusions until one has enough facts to back them up. In this case, I don't know enough about the background to offer an opinion.'

'Oh, come on, Malk. You know as much about the background as anyone in Fethering.'

'Maybe I did once,' he said, rather primly, 'but I'm retired now.'

'The events we're talking about occurred long before you were retired.'

'I thought we were talking about Harry Lasalle's death. That only happened yesterday.'

Carole looked at the old journalist beadily, certain that he was being deliberately obtuse. 'What I am interested in is the cause of Harry Lasalle's death.'

'I thought the consensus on that was carbon monoxide poisoning.'

'Malk, you know what I mean.'

'I'm afraid I don't.' He took refuge in a long swallow of coffee.

'When we met before,' Carole persisted, 'when I asked you about possible relationships Anita Garner might have had while she was working at Footscrow House, you talked in general terms about the common phenomenon of bosses "coming on" – with impunity – to members of their staff.'

'Did I? I really don't remember.' He suddenly sounded very old and confused. Carole felt convinced, however, that it was a ploy to make her back off.

And she wasn't about to fall for it. 'Were there any rumours back then of Harry Lasalle "coming on" to his staff?'

Malk Penberthy physically squirmed with discomfort. 'As I said, such allegations are made about the bosses in any organization. But there was not so much publicity about that kind of thing back then. Women were conditioned to be less assertive. No junior employee would have contemplated taking a senior member of staff to court for sexual harassment . . . even for rape. Incidents like that got covered up. The complainant would just be moved to another job. In those days, a boss with wandering hands could get away with murder.'

His expression showed he'd just realized the implication of his words.

Carole rubbed it in. 'Unfortunate thing to say . . . given the circumstances.'

'Maybe.' He looked appropriately cowed.

'So, Malk, all I'm asking is . . . At the time of Anita Garner's disappearance, was there talk of Harry Lasalle having "come on" to her – or even of their being in a relationship?'

'There was all kinds of talk round that time . . . as you can imagine in a place like Fethering.' He was silent.

'That doesn't answer my question,' Carole prompted.

'No.'

'Were there actual accusations of sexual harassment levelled at Harry Lasalle?'

Another silence. Then, 'All right, yes, there were. A couple of the other younger care staff claimed that Harry had . . . touched them up.'

'And did they say whether he'd done the same to Anita?'

'I don't think they had any proof of it, but they suggested it was likely that he had. Listen,' he pleaded, 'these were two young girls, still in their teens, and suddenly they're the centre of media attention . . . not just me from the *Fethering Observer*, but the nationals were briefly interested in Anita Garner's disappearance. Radio reporters, television crews. So, these kids loved their moment in the spotlight, and they probably embellished their stories to keep the focus on themselves. They told the national press what the national press wanted to hear.'

'Which was?'

'That Harry Lasalle had done more than "come on" to Anita Garner. That they were in a relationship. That she was his mistress.'

'And do you think that was true?'

'Absolutely not!' The old man looked affronted by the very suggestion. 'All right, Harry's "wandering hands" may have wandered where they shouldn't, but I'm sure it didn't go further than that. What the girls said was just fabrication and rumours.'

'Presumably fabrication and rumours that the police would have followed up on?'

'Presumably.'

'Did you hear their conclusions?'

Malk Penberthy smiled wryly, 'No, I'm sorry to say I didn't. In detective stories, the police seem to be very generous sharing all their findings with amateur sleuths. Real life, I believe, is rather different . . . not least because amateur sleuths do not exist. They are a complete and convenient figment of crime writers' imaginations.

'And I'm afraid the same holds true for the relationship between the press and the police. Again, in fiction, the latter are far more open-handed with information than they are in the real world. Journalists in books always seem to have a friendly source in the police force who keeps them up to date with the progress of their enquiries. Whereas, in the real world, journalists are fed what the police want them to know at press conferences. Apart from that, the "appropriate authorities" tend to play things rather close to their chests. So, the detectives looking into Anita Garner's disappearance – surprise, surprise – did not go out of their way to confide in me the results of their investigation into the relationship between Harry Lasalle and the missing girl.'

'No, Malk, but you must have been talking to lots of other people, apart from the police. You must have formed your own opinion on the subject.'

'Yes, that's true. And I did briefly entertain the idea that the two might be involved in some ongoing affair.'

'"Briefly"?'

'Yes. Because I soon found out that, whatever was the cause of Anita's disappearance, her murder or any other outcome, Harry Lasalle could not have had anything to do with it.'

'Oh?'

'He had an alibi for the relevant days. He was with his wife Veronica, on a sailing trip to Northern France in his boat.'

'*Harry's Dream*?'

'The very same.'

'So, the police would have found out about that alibi too?'

'I can only assume so. Once again, they were not magnanimous enough to vouchsafe me that information.'

'Ah. Right.'

Carole must have looked as crestfallen as she felt, because

Malk Penberthy said, 'I'm sorry. I can only wish you better luck
with your investigation than I had with mine.'

'Thanks,' said Carole ruefully.

He looked at his watch. 'I must be on my way.'

'Oh?'

'I'm due to do a guided tour of the Fedborough Wetlands
Centre.'

'Ah.'

'Birding has always been a big thing with me.'

'More coffee?'

Jude had just come back in from her walk. It had done the
business. Her body, underneath its many layers, felt warm again.
But she was glad to be back in the central heating of Woodside
Cottage.

'Never say no to a cup of coffee,' said Pete. 'My drug of
choice. Need constant fixes.'

Jude went through to the kitchen to put the kettle on and
called back, 'While I was out, I was thinking about Harry
Lasalle.'

'Me, and all. Felt sorry for the old bugger. He sounded so
down on Saturday. Wondered whether I should have said something or, I don't know, called Veronica to ask her to look out for
him.'

'We weren't to know what would happen.'

'No, you're right.' Pete had reached the stage of sanding down
uneven bumps on the sitting-room wall.

'I was asking myself whether I should feel guilty about what
happened and decided I shouldn't.'

'But why should you feel guilty, Jude? You only met Harry
on Saturday.'

'Yes, but, if he did take his own life . . . and if that was because
people had started talking about Anita Garner again . . . Here.
White with one sugar.'

Pete took the proffered cup. 'Thank you. Still don't see what
it's got to do with you.'

'Well, I was the one who took Anita Garner's handbag to
the police station, and that's what started everyone talking about
her.'

'You was just doing your civic duty, Jude. A public-spirited act. Nothing to feel guilty about.'

She still couldn't quite convince herself. If she and Carole hadn't started "stirring things up" again . . .

'Pete, were you aware of any talk about something going on between Anita and Harry Lasalle?'

But he wasn't to be drawn. 'There's always talk about stuff like that. After she went, the poor kid's name was linked to virtually everyone in Fethering.'

'Including you?' asked Jude cheekily.

The decorator grinned. 'Probably. It's always a problem when what's being talked about is something nobody knows a blind thing about. Not, of course, that ignorance of the facts has ever stopped the gossips of Fethering.'

'True.' Jude took a sip of her coffee. It continued the warming-up process.

'They come up with more theories than you've had hot dinners,' Pete continued. 'Particularly when the subject might be murder. Generally speaking, I reckon the people of Fethering spend far too much time watching television. That's where they get all their theories from. If you ask me, there's too much bloody crime on television. Particularly now there's all that forensic stuff. People used to watch the box to learn how to cook. Then they started on decorating, house makeovers, all that . . . which, let me tell you, didn't help me doing my job. Nothing worse than a client who reckons they know how to do it better than I do. "Ooh, on the telly, they were doing this rag-rolling and they were using stencils and they . . ." If they're so clever, why don't they just bloody get on with it, rather than bringing me in just to listen to their criticism?'

For a moment, Pete sounded uncharacteristically angry, but then he relaxed into the familiar grin. 'Anyway, now everyone watches so much bloody forensics on telly, half of them reckon they could conduct their own post-mortems. As I say, too much crime, people think they know it all.'

'Of course,' said Jude, 'one of the clichés of crime on telly, and in books, is the old theory that the first suspect is always the person who finds the body.'

'Oh yes, I've heard that one a few times.'

'So, Pete, you said it was someone from Fethering Yacht Club who went out and found *Harry's Dream* on Sunday.'

'Right.'

'Who was it?'

'Glen Porter,' said the decorator.

EIGHT

I t was Jude's suggestion that they should go for an early evening drink at the Crown and Anchor. The weather was so miserable, with icy rain sheeting down from the dark heavens, that she wanted the comfort of sitting by an open fire. She couldn't do that at Woodside Cottage because Pete had covered all the furniture with paint-spattered sheets. As for open fires at High Tor . . . well, they only happened when its owner had guests. And Jude was too frequent a visitor to count as a guest.

When they arrived at the pub, unsurprisingly, Barney Poulton was generating conversation . . . or no, 'conversation' implies a two-way process, and he didn't go in for that. The fact that no one in the bar was taking any notice did not deter him one iota. While he pontificated, Jude went up to the bar and ordered two large New Zealand Sauvignon Blancs from Zosia, Ted Crisp's Polish bar manager.

Of course, Barney was talking about the death of Harry Lasalle. Though he was not a member of Fethering Yacht Club, he had many golfing friends who were, so he felt confident of his facts. (When do the Barney Poultons of this life *not* feel confident of their facts?)

'Obviously, it's related to the Anita Garner case. From the moment that handbag was discovered at Fiasco House' – Barney was very punctilious about using Fethering local patois – 'he knew he was on borrowed time. The revived investigation into the girl's disappearance was going to end up on his doorstep sooner or later.

'Harry Lasalle's suicide couldn't be a clearer admission of guilt. Now it's just a matter of the police tracking down where he hid the body. My instinct is still that it's somewhere up on the South Downs . . . shallow grave, you know. I've known Anita Garner was murdered from the moment I first heard about the case.'

Though unwilling to get involved in conversation with Barney

Poulton, Carole couldn't help herself from asking, 'And when was it you first heard about the case? We're talking about events thirty years ago, and you've been in Fethering . . . what? Four years?'

'Nearly five,' he said, somewhat piqued. 'And since I've been here, I have made it my business to find out everything I can about the village.'

Carole should have realized. Barney Poulton was like the Wobbly Man her son Stephen had played with as a child. However many times you pushed him down, he still sprang right back up again.

Returning with the drinks, Jude thought it worth seeing whether Barney might actually have some useful information. 'Terribly sad about Harry,' she said. 'Have you heard any more details about it . . . you know, round the yacht club?'

She knew full well that Barney Poulton wasn't a member and he was forced to admit as much. But he quickly bounced back. 'A lot of my golfing friends are members there, though, so I have heard a bit of the inside stuff.'

Of course, thought Jude. It went against Barney's principles ever to admit ignorance about anything.

'It was Glen Porter who went out in search of *Harry's Dream*, wasn't it?' she prompted.

'Yes, that's right.'

'You know him, don't you?' she asked casually.

'Not well.' For which, when it's Barney Poulton talking, read: Hardly at all.

'You said you played golf with him.'

'Yes. Well, we're members of the same golf club.' Barney was backing off. The close relationship he'd earlier implied that he had with Glen Porter was perhaps not so close when it came under scrutiny. 'He travels a lot. And keeps himself to himself when he's here in Fethering. In fact, it's interesting what happened to him. He unexpectedly came into a lot of money when—'

'We know all about that,' said Carole tartly.

'Oh.' But it was only a momentary diversion from the vertical as the Wobbly Man bounced back. 'He doesn't work at all, Glen Porter, you know.'

'Yes, we do,' said Carole in the same tone as before.

She could see that he was desperate to come up with something they hadn't heard before. Anything. And, of course, according to Barney Poulton's scale of values, it didn't have to be something true.

'It's an open secret,' he said confidentially, 'that there was history between Glen and Anita Garner . . .'

'Oh?'

'They were at school together . . .' Carole couldn't be bothered to say that they knew that too. 'And Glen was a bit of a Jack-the-Lad back then. Good-looking and he knew it. Worked his way through most of the girls in his year.'

'Including Anita Garner?' suggested Jude.

'More than likely,' said Barney Poulton sagely. 'So, you see, when she started working at Fiasco House and Harry Lasalle came on to her . . . well, Glen's nose might have been put out of joint . . .'

'Are you implying,' asked Carole sharply, 'that Glen Porter might have killed Harry Lasalle?'

But that was a step too far for Barney. He didn't mind insinuating, but he'd stop short of accusing. 'I'm just saying that is a possible theory that's going around among the more gossipy denizens of Fethering.'

Huh, thought Jude. Takes one to know one. Be hard pushed to find anyone more gossipy than you.

'And there's another theory that—'

His further theorizing was stopped by Ted Crisp, issuing out of the kitchen area into the bar. 'You've come out without your phone again, Barney.'

'What?'

'Your wife just rang, wanting to know where the hell you are. Have you forgotten you've got – her words – "a bloody bridge game at seven"?'

'Oh, damn. Yes, I must go.'

He scurried out of the bar, looking less like 'the eyes and ears of Fethering', more like an old-fashioned henpecked husband. And somehow his image of the horny-handed depository of village folklore was undermined by the fact that he played that most middle-class of games, bridge.

The landlord watched him go, then said to Carole and Jude, 'I think I might use that one again.'

'What?' asked Jude.

'Telling him the missus had been on the phone.'

'What, wasn't she?' asked Carole. 'Did you make it up?'

'Not this time I didn't, no. But seeing the speed with which he scarpered at the summons from home, I might resort to that tactic on one of the many occasions when I can't stand listening to another bloody word from him.'

'Certainly worth trying,' said Jude.

'Was he going on about Anita Garner again?' asked Ted.

'Barney? Oh yes.'

'Him and his bloody theories.'

'You got any new thoughts on it?' asked Carole.

'Why should I have? You know full well it all happened years before I took over the Crown and Anchor. Before I'd even heard of Fethering.'

'Yes, I do know that. But, standing behind your bar, you do hear a lot of gossip.'

'I hear it, but I don't listen. Manage to tune it out mostly.'

'So, no new theories?'

'Nope. Plenty of rehashing of old ones.'

'Hm.'

'Actually, I wanted to have a word with you two . . .'

'Oh, yes?'

'Ask your advice, as it were. Pick your brains.'

Jude grinned. 'You're welcome to anything you can find there.'

'Right.' Ted Crisp paused, rather more momentously than was his custom. Then he asked, 'Do you think it'd be a good idea for me to have a vegan menu here at the Crown and Anchor?'

'Ted Crisp talking about veganism? I didn't think he even knew what veganism was. What on earth's going on, Jude?'

They were walking back from the pub. It wasn't actually raining but the air felt damp, clinging and icy.

'I think it might be the company he's been keeping,' Jude suggested.

'But Ted doesn't keep any company. Just the staff at the pub.'

'Ah. Well, he took someone out to lunch the other day. At a vegan restaurant in Brighton.'

'Who? Who on earth would he be taking out to lunch?'

Jude told her. Carole was surprised how much it hurt. A long time ago, in a distant world of unlikely events, Carole Seddon and Ted Crisp had had a brief affair. It hadn't lasted. Their expectations of what life might offer, their expectations of each other, were so different, it couldn't have lasted.

And Carole thought she'd put it completely behind her, with a mixture of embarrassment and a slight *frisson* at the recollection that she could still interest a man in that way.

But she felt disturbed and undermined by the fact that the landlord was now showing interest in another woman.

Or maybe what upset her was that the woman in question was Brandie Neville, an aspirant healer.

Jude had a strong belief in synchronicity. Not a subject she raised in Carole's presence, to avoid the inevitable derision it would prompt.

So, given the fact that they'd been discussing Glen Porter in the Crown and Anchor, she was totally unsurprised to come back to Woodside Cottage and find a message from him on the answering machine.

She rang back immediately.

'Hello?' The greeting was cautious.

'This is Jude. You left me a message.'

'Ah yes. I wonder if we could meet . . .?'

This was going better than she dared hope. 'That would be fine.'

'You live in Fethering – is that right?'

'Yes.'

'I wonder . . . would you be able to join me for a cup of coffee tomorrow morning at about eleven?'

'I could do that. What – Starbucks?'

'Do you actually like Starbucks?'

'No.'

'I don't think anyone does. Its success is one of the unsolved mysteries of the last fifty years.'

'You could be right.'

'Well, Jude, since neither of us likes Starbucks . . . and Fethering doesn't boast one of those friendly one-off coffee shops beloved of American sitcoms, I'm suggesting that you join me for coffee at my beach hut. That's on Fethering Beach.'

'I know the one. I've walked past it many times.'

'Eleven o'clock tomorrow morning then?'

'That'll be fine.'

There are women who might have been cautious about fixing a meeting alone with a man who featured high on their list of murder suspects. But Jude wasn't one of them.

Coming down the next morning to find the decorator already painting away, as she put the kettle on for her tea and his coffee, she didn't mention her upcoming tryst. But she did raise the name of Glen Porter. 'Were you at the same school as him, Pete?'

'Yes. Went to the same primary. Only one in Fethering. Mind you, I'm a few years older. Didn't know him at school.'

'And how well do you know him now?'

Pete shrugged. 'To say hello. If I see him down the yacht club. Like we did on Saturday. But I don't see him that often. He travels a lot.'

'So I've heard. Just for pleasure?'

'Guess so. Certainly no one's ever heard of him doing any work. Still, maybe if I could afford it, I'd do the same.'

'And he has a reputation as a bit of a lady's man, I've heard.'

'Did have, apparently. Though we're talking a long time ago. When he was at school and in his early twenties. Haven't heard so much about the lady's man stuff since he came into Reefer Townsend's money. Still, maybe that's what Glen gets up to on his travels. A woman in every international resort . . .? I really don't know.'

'He's never been married?'

'Don't think so.'

'And no current relationships round Fethering?'

'Not as far as I know.'

'Hm.' Jude shivered. 'Feels a bit cold down here to me. I'm going to take my cup of tea up to bed.'

*   *   *

From an upstairs window at High Tor, Carole saw her neighbour setting out from Woodside Cottage at about half ten. She couldn't suppress a tickle of curiosity about where Jude might be going. No planned excursion had been mentioned in the Crown and Anchor the evening before.

Maybe it was a client . . .? Having the sitting room decorated ruled out seeing the deluded and hypochondriac of Fethering in her usual workspace . . . and Jude had talked about visiting some clients in their own homes . . . Yes, that was a possible scenario.

But Carole concluded it was more likely her neighbour was going to visit another of the lovers she'd kept quiet about.

Of course, there was no way she was going to feel jealous about the situation. Having had as many lovers as Jude had was, to Carole's mind, definite proof of neediness and mental instability.

And she herself had far too many other priorities in her life to worry about men. Carole had always felt rather sorry for women whose whole identity was predicated on having a man around. Granted, her own track record in that area had not been particularly distinguished. Her marriage to David had ended in divorce. And her other major romantic excursion, with Ted Crisp, had been . . . well . . .

And now that same Ted Crisp had the nerve to be planning vegan menus with Brandie Neville!

Carole's seething fury knew no bounds.

The impression Jude had got from the exterior of Glen Porter's beach hut – that it looked Chekhovian – was reinforced by being inside. The seasoned wooden rafters had faded to grey and the low slopes of the ceilings gave the feeling of a pre-revolutionary *dacha*. The view the leaded windows afforded on to the English Channel felt somehow wrong. The building's rightful place was in a forest clearing, preferably blanketed with snow.

Though the place had not been modernized, it had been punc-tiliously maintained. Many beach huts are kept in a state of casual scruffiness, seaside equipment left out for easy access and the basic principle of cleanliness being, 'Well, since everything's going to get covered with sand, anyway . . .' Not in this beach hut, though. Any surface that should have been polished gleamed

with recent ministrations, and not a single cobweb had been
allowed to secrete itself behind a rafter. Since Glen Porter himself
did not have the air of a do-it-yourself cleaner, he must have had
a highly efficient team on the job. But presumably, Jude surmised,
if money's no object . . .

She wasn't quite sure what she had been expecting from
meeting Glen, but he didn't conform to any of the obvious
stereotypes. He certainly didn't demonstrate the flamboyance
implied in Barney Poulton's assertion that he could just 'splash
the cash'. Glen was dressed in well-cut leisurewear but nothing
extravagant. And, though the beach hut was well looked after,
there was no evidence of excessive expenditure on the décor and
set dressing.

As for the vaunted Jack-the-Laddishness, that seemed to have
been toned down too, possibly just with maturity. Jude was
accorded a look of quiet appreciation, acknowledgement that she
was an attractive woman, but nothing more overt than that.

For herself, she could recognize his attractiveness, but it wasn't
the kind that threatened her equilibrium. Behind the long grey
hair and the laid-back leisurewear, she could detect in his manner
a detached canniness, a level of calculation. It was a personality
trait that, she knew, could quickly flip into intransigence.

He prepared their coffee – needless to say he had the latest
machine, which did the full grind-to-pour routine – in the kitchen,
calling through casual pleasantries about the ghastly weather.
Jude sat on the comfortable tweed sofa on to which she had been
directed. Her anticipation was tinged with excitement. She felt
sure Glen Porter had something to tell her about the death of
Harry Lasalle . . . which might well lead to information about
the disappearance of Anita Garner.

'This is a fabulous building,' she said, as he came back into
the sitting room. 'Fabulous position.'

'Yes. You're not the only person to think that.'

'Oh?'

'A lot of people want to buy it off me.' Having placed her
coffee – in a nice bone-china cup and saucer – on the table next
to the sofa, he took a seat in the armchair opposite. 'Latest,' he
went on, 'is Roland Lasalle, the *property developer*.' He put a
lot of unexplained irony into the last two words. 'He'd like to

turn it into a swish restaurant, to cater to all the people who he hopes will be filling out the holiday flatlets he's making at Footscrow House.'

'And are you interested?'

'Why should I be?'

'If he made you a big enough offer . . .?'

'I don't need money,' said Glen, in a way that somehow closed the subject.

He took a sip of coffee, put the cup and saucer down firmly and focused his eyes on hers. He was as aware of the serious nature of their encounter as she was.

'Right,' he said. 'Let's get a bit of clarity into things, shall we?'

'What things?' asked Jude, with deliberate *faux* naivety.

He smiled wryly, recognizing the game she was playing. 'Let's say that you and your friend Carole have been digging into things that don't concern you.'

'How do you define "concern"?'

'Things that aren't your business.'

'That's just saying the same thing in other words. You may not think it's our business – or concern, come to that – but we clearly feel differently.'

'Why? Your motivation is basically nosiness. You've got time on your hands, so you get involved in other people's business . . . regardless of what harm that might do to the other people concerned.'

'Glen, you said we needed clarity. It might help then if we were clear about who is actually involved, who might be hurt by our investigations.'

He didn't answer her direct enquiry by coming up with names. Instead, he looked straight into Jude's brown eyes and said, 'I'm assuming that you and your friend don't get pleasure from causing pain to other people . . .?'

Jude could have come up with an angry response to that, but instead she just said evenly, 'You assume correctly.'

'So, why do you go to such efforts to try to expose people's secrets?'

'Because . . .' Jude sighed. 'This is going to sound very pious, I'm afraid, but it's because we don't like seeing injustice done.

And we don't feel so bad about causing pain to people who have caused pain to others.'

'Hm. Very neat. And, as you say, pious.'

'It's hard to explain without sounding pious.'

'Hm.' He took a long swallow of coffee. 'And where are your pious enquiries directing you at the moment?'

'Carole and I think the timing of Harry Lasalle's death was rather suspicious.'

'Interesting.' Was Jude being fanciful to see a slight relaxation of tension in Glen Porter's face?

'How much do you know about how Harry died?' he asked.

'We know that he was found dead in his boat, *Harry's Dream*. In fact, we know that you were the one who found him dead in *Harry's Dream*.'

'I see.' Another crooked grin. 'And, following the hackneyed crime fiction trope that the person who finds the body is always the first suspect . . .?'

Jude was annoyed to feel herself blushing. She was also aware that Glen Porter was very much running the interview. He had summoned her to his beachside stronghold and he was dictating the terms of their conversation. He was also revealing himself to be much more intelligent and articulate than she had expected.

'I suppose that might be a view,' she said. It was not nearly as strong a response as she had wanted.

'Do you, incidentally,' asked Glen, 'know what caused Harry Lasalle's death?'

'I heard from Pete the decorator that it was carbon monoxide poisoning.'

'Pete the decorator was right. And do you know how carbon monoxide poisoning works?'

'Pretty much, I'd say. Not the chemical or biological details but, basically, it chokes you, doesn't it?'

'Yes, that's about right. You die of asphyxiation. But it does take a long time for the gas to build up.'

'So?'

'So, if you wanted to examine your theory about me being the first suspect for murdering him because I was first out to *Harry's Dream*, let's go through what I would have had to do.

I would have had to get out to the boat in my own boat, board it, sabotage the heating system while Harry wasn't watching, make idle chatter for what . . . an hour maybe, while he drank himself insensible . . . and then make sure that he was lying down in the lowest part of the boat so that the carbon monoxide could do its stuff. I'd have to watch him choke to death . . . while ensuring that I didn't succumb to the carbon monoxide myself, and then what? Go back on my own boat to Fethering Yacht Club to raise the alarm? Would you call that a likely scenario?'

Jude was forced to concede that she wouldn't.

'And if I didn't do that,' Glen Porter pushed on, 'do you think anyone else is likely to have done it?'

'No,' a shamefaced Jude agreed.

'So, we're back to two other possibilities, aren't we? Either poor old Harry died as a result of an accident or . . . he topped himself. Not being of a romantic or fanciful nature, I favour the accident.'

'Hm.'

'You sound disappointed.'

'Maybe. A little.'

'All right then, Jude . . . following the more romantic or fanciful theory . . . why would a harmless old codger like Harry want to top himself?'

'Perhaps there was some secret he wanted to keep hidden and he knew it was about to be revealed.'

'What secret?'

'Something that would disgrace him . . . or get him in trouble with the police, maybe?'

Glen Porter's mouth twisted with scepticism. 'I don't think much of that as a theory.'

'Nor do I,' said Jude, with renewed spirit. 'In fact, I much prefer my murder scenario.'

'Oh God.' A wry smile. 'Not with me still featuring at the top of the cast list, I hope?'

'Maybe not. But murder makes the stakes higher.'

'Inevitably. I come back, though, to a rather similar question to the one I recently voiced. Why would anyone want to murder a harmless old codger like Harry?'

'Perhaps because, yes, he did have a secret. But it was a secret whose revelation didn't threaten him. It threatened someone else.'

'So that someone else killed him to keep him quiet?'

'Makes sense to me.'

'I don't think it'd make much sense in a court of law, Jude. Depending, of course, on what Harry Lasalle's combustible secret was. I don't suppose, by any chance, you know, do you?'

She could only admit another 'No'.

Once again, she sensed relief in his reaction.

'So, I suppose, Jude, in your alternative scenarios . . . be it suicide or murder . . . the secret that Harry Lasalle was either trying to keep quiet or have kept quiet by someone else . . . there was a woman involved?'

'Yes. I think there was.'

'A woman who would be hurt by the revelation, in whichever direction that revelation went?'

She nodded. 'That's the way my thoughts have been moving.'

'So, the motive for the murder – or suicide – was to protect that woman?'

'Well, I think we ought to get clear who—'

Glen Porter was interrupted by a tap at the door. He looked up in some surprise. Jude got the impression he didn't expect unscheduled visitors at his beach hut, that it was his private space.

An even greater surprise was that the door was then pushed open to reveal Lauren Givens standing there. She was smartly dressed and carefully made-up. Smiling. But her expression changed instantly when she saw Jude.

'Oh, hello, Glen,' she said. She looked down to her hand, which held one of the flyers for her Pottery Open Day. 'Do come along to this tomorrow if you get the time.'

She placed the flyer on a table, turned tail and hurried out, closing the door behind her.

Glen Porter suddenly had an urgent meeting he had to be at rather soon. Jude was quickly and unceremoniously hustled out of the beach hut.

As she passed through the doorway, she breathed in the intensity of Lauren Givens's perfume.

*　　*　　*

Jude walked slowly back across Fethering Beach. She remembered when she had surprised Lauren on the sand the previous Thursday. She thought back to the Saturday morning in Fethering Yacht Club. She had thought Glen Porter had hurried out so soon after arriving because he'd seen Harry Lasalle. Wasn't it just as possible that he'd seen Lauren Givens, sitting with her husband? And then there was the way Lauren and Glen had behaved at his beach hut that morning . . .

Jude had been a keen observer of human behaviour for quite a while. And she recognized instinctively the signs of a couple pretending that they weren't having an affair.

NINE

Carole's sour mood was somewhat sweetened by a call from Malk Penberthy, suggesting another meeting over coffee in Starbucks.

He must have news to impart. News which he probably could have imparted over the phone. But Carole preferred the idea of face-to-face contact. She thought it might be a symptom of loneliness in the old man but found that endearing rather than worrying. She also once again relished the idea of something covert, having her own private source of information.

And she was, in part, relieved. There had been some asperity in their meeting on the Monday, with her pushing Malk for revelations he was unwilling to share, and she was comforted that that hadn't led to a permanent rift.

Their encounter that morning followed the previously established format of not getting to the meat of their subject until they were both supplied with coffees and had exchanged pleasantries about the inclemency of the weather.

'I have been making it my business,' Malk began in his customary formal manner, 'to elicit information about the late Harry Lasalle's involvement in the various incarnations of Footscrow House . . . or, as you probably know, what is known to the Fethering cognoscenti as "Fiasco House".'

'I have heard it called that, yes.'

'Well, Carole, you may also know that the building is currently being converted into holiday flatlets.' She nodded. 'Maybe a project which will finally turn the fortunes of the place into something profitable.'

'Maybe.' She was keen for him to get through the preamble and tell her his latest discovery. But she was too well brought up to push him. Let him tell his story at a pace of his own choosing.

'Now, in the past, Harry Lasalle kind of dabbled as a property developer. He started out as a builder, just that, and was very successful at it. Made a lot of money out of Lasalle Build and Design and started to think, "Why should I just be employed by other people to build houses which they're going to sell at high profit? Why shouldn't I be working on my own projects, so that I get a bit of that money too?"

'He had variable success. Made money on some developments, lost on others. Only one thing remained constant – whenever he got involved with Fiasco House, it was the Midas touch in reverse. Sheer disaster. Maybe nobody could ever have made that place profitable. Certainly, Harry Lasalle couldn't.

'Meanwhile, he – or even more his wife Veronica – was grooming their son Roland to be an entirely different kind of operator, rather in the way thuggish homicidal Mafia bosses are supposed to get their sons trained up as lawyers. Roland Lasalle's dainty hands would never be allowed to get engrained with cement dust like his father's. He was a professional man, an architect, not a builder. Public school education, university, architect's training, membership of London clubs – a precision-cut diamond, while his father was a rough one.

'So, Roland was trained to have the social skills and articulacy which would make him a much more effective property developer than his father. For many of his projects, the younger Lasalle relied on investment from Harry, but in no way was it an equal partnership. The father was back in his box, working for someone else, though now the one who was raking in the big profits was his own son.

'On the latest development, though, the conversion of Footscrow House into holiday flatlets, Roland has totally cut his father out. Raised the money elsewhere, wouldn't allow Harry to invest. Employed other builders, cut out Lasalle Build and Design completely. Which, from all accounts, the old man took very badly.

'So, Carole, I was thinking that might be of interest to you . . . another factor for you and your friend to consider in your investigation.'

She had never actually spelled out what she and Jude were investigating, or even that they were investigating anything, but clearly Malk Penberthy had deduced it for himself. Or maybe, given the way gossip travelled in Fethering, someone else had told him what they were up to.

'Malk,' Carole began slowly, 'I'm really grateful to you for telling me that. It does open out a lot of new possibilities.'

'I agree. Certainly, if one were going down the route of believing that Harry Lasalle's death was suicide, that might give him an additional motive. It's entirely possible he would have regarded his son's behaviour as a betrayal. And if the old man had health problems, if his body was starting to let him down, that might be a stark reminder that he could no longer sustain the lifestyle that he was used to. Roland might have delivered to him a rather brutal form of *memento mori*. People, I am aware, have committed suicide with less reason.'

'Yes,' said Carole thoughtfully. She was trying to piece together how this rift between father and son might fit into a scenario in which Harry's death was murder. But maybe she needed a bit more background first . . .?

'Malk,' she began tentatively, 'going back a bit . . .'

'Hm?'

'Back to the time of Anita Garner's disappearance . . .'

'Yes.' A slight smile played around his thin lips, as if he were acknowledging the predictability of her redirection.

'Do you know the detail of Harry Lasalle's involvement with Footscrow House back then?'

'Well, he owned it. And he ran it as a care home, with his wife Veronica. Not very successfully. That's why, soon after, he cut his losses and converted the place into a boutique hotel. Which – surprise, surprise – wasn't very successful either.'

'So, Malk, going back to Anita Garner's handbag, why was the bedroom where it was found being decorated at the time? To improve the conditions of the care home?'

'By no means. Harry was already running the care home business down, looking to Fiasco House's next incarnation as a hotel. He wasn't replacing residents who died off and he was working with the local authorities to get the remaining ones transferred to other local homes.'

'So, the bedroom was being redecorated for its new life as a hotel room?'

'Precisely that, Carole.'

'And Harry and his firm wouldn't have been doing the decoration themselves?'

'No. He was basically a builder. He always subcontracted decorating jobs.'

'And do you know who he subcontracted that one to?'

Malk Penberthy let out a little smile which seemed to say that Carole wasn't going to catch him out in ignorance that easily. 'Yes, he gave the job to Brenton Wilkinson.'

'The decorator who Pete used to work for before he set up on his own?'

'That's right.'

'Is he still around?'

'Brenton? Just about.'

'He must be very old.'

'He's exactly the same age as I am,' said Malk Penberthy rather tartly.

'Oh, I'm sorry.'

'Don't worry. I long ago gave up all attempts to pass myself off as a spring chicken.' His tone was joking but he still looked hurt.

'And do I gather that you know Brenton Wilkinson?'

'I do.'

'I don't suppose, Malk . . . it would be possible for . . .'

'To introduce you to Brenton?'

'Yes,' she admitted.

The former journalist grinned. 'I think that could be arranged.'

Jude didn't have a problem with Pete being in the house, but there were one or two phone calls that discretion told her were better taken upstairs. His hearing details of her private life didn't worry her too much, but she thought Pete himself might be embarrassed.

On the Wednesday morning, she was downstairs in her robe, chatting to the decorator, when the phone rang. Seeing on the screen who it was, she decided to take the phone up to her bedroom.

Ted Crisp. What was all this with Ted Crisp ringing her? He'd only ever rung her before in an emergency or to make the briefest of arrangements. And now suddenly he wants to share with her far more than she might have wished.

It was about Brandie again. Of course. The landlord had clearly got it bad.

'I was wondering . . .' Ted said tentatively – and tentative was far from his natural style. 'I was wondering whether you could give me some advice . . .?'

'Of course,' said Jude, sitting on the bed and wrapping the double duvet around her shoulders. Though the central heating was on full blast, the house still felt cold. It was that marooned time in February when even the idea of summer was a cruel illusion.

'Well,' the landlord went on, still not finding progress easy, 'you know, in the past, I may sometimes have sounded a bit . . . well, sceptical about some of your ideas, Jude . . .'

'Ideas like healing and alternative therapies and what Carole would call "mumbo-jumbo" . . .?' Jude offered helpfully.

'That sort of thing, yes.'

'Yes, I have noticed that, Ted.'

'Ah.'

'It was when you said things like "I had a pain in my foot, so I went to a heeler. He put new soles on too while he was at it." Up to the usual standard of your jokes, but it made me think perhaps you didn't take what I did seriously.'

'I'm sorry, Jude. I apologize.'

'Bit late for that.'

'Oh,' he wheedled, 'you can't judge a man by his jokes.'

'Just as well in your case, Ted,' said Jude with a grin in her voice. 'What a mercy it was to the stand-up comedy circuit when you gave it up.'

'I agree, I agree. There are lots of things I've done in the past that I regret bitterly.'

'Don't be too hard on yourself.'

'No, but, Jude, I realize I've spent all my life . . . "not giving space for my spiritual dimension".'

That sounded very much like a quote. And Jude didn't have any doubt about who he was quoting. 'How is Brandie, by the way, Ted?'

'Well, she's . . . Well, she's . . .' But encapsulating his feelings in words was a feat beyond him. 'I enjoy her company,' he concluded formally.

'Good.'

'But I do feel . . . I don't know . . . unworthy of her.'

'"Unworthy"?'

'Yes. Brandie's so much younger than me . . . but so much wiser.'

'"Wiser"?' Jude realized this was a conversation in which her role was in danger of being reduced to that of an echo.

'Yes,' Ted Crisp confirmed. 'Brandie has a wisdom that is as old as all of history.'

Jude thought the safest response to this was silence. Any other options would have involved giggling.

'And I was wondering, Jude . . .' Ted went on.

'Yes?'

'. . . whether you could help me find space for my spiritual dimension?'

Jude was dressed and getting Pete yet another cup of coffee (white with one sugar), when the knocker sounded. She opened the front door to reveal a woman whose expression was as wintry as the blast of cold air she brought in.

Jude had seen her before around Fethering but they'd never exchanged words. She thought she knew who the woman was, though, and this was confirmed by the announcement, 'I'm Veronica Lasalle. I need to talk to you.'

Jude's gesture of welcome was too late, Harry Lasalle's widow was already in the house, closing the front door behind her. She was a short woman with harsh features, zipped into a hooded purple puffa jacket. The hair that was visible had once been reddish and had paled into a kind of sandy white. She moved as though her knees were giving her pain.

'Good morning, Pete,' she said.

The decorator's reaction was unexpected. After an automatic 'Good morning, Veronica', he started to wrap his brushes in damp cloths, before saying he needed to get to the trade counter for some more paint. His aversion to being in the same space as Veronica Lasalle could not have been more clumsily disguised.

Bewildered by this uncharacteristic brusqueness, Jude offered her visitor tea or coffee.

'No. I haven't come to socialize. I've come to talk to you.'

'Well, at least sit down.' Jude gestured to sheet-shrouded sitting-room furniture. 'There are chairs in the kitchen if you—'

'I'll stand. If I sit down for too long, my arthritis seizes up.'

'Right.' Jude didn't feel she could sit down if her guest wasn't doing so. She stood awkwardly facing the woman and said, 'I was very sorry to hear the news about your husband's death.'

'Were you?' The response was almost snapped. 'Well, of course, that's what everyone says in circumstances like this, don't they?'

'Perhaps, but I—'

'Anyway, I haven't come here for your sympathy. I've come to find out what rumours you have been spreading about Harry.'

'I can assure you I haven't been—'

'You're the one who found the handbag at Footscrow House, aren't you?'

'I was with Pete when he found it, yes.'

'Yes, but you're the one who's been digging up the past, all those rumours about Harry and Anita Garner.'

'I wouldn't say I've been—'

'You and that skinny neighbour of yours, Carole Seddon.'

'We—'

'Well, I hope you're happy with what your meddling has achieved.'

'I don't know—'

'Harry could have had a good few more years of happy life if you hadn't stirred things up.'

Jude didn't say anything. She knew she'd only be interrupted.

'It was all untrue,' Veronica went on, 'what they said back then but, of course, mud sticks, doesn't it? Especially in a little place like Fethering. Harry's always been good to his workforce, whatever business he's been in. And it was like that when we was running Footscrow House as a care home. Yes, he was friendly to Anita, but he was friendly to all the younger ones, tried to make them feel at home. He knew the job they was doing could be tough and he liked them to feel he was someone they could bring their troubles to – a shoulder to cry on, if you like. But that's as far as it went – with Anita or any other of the girls, come to that. I was living in the building, helping him run the place. I'd have known if there was any hanky-panky going on. But once people like you start to gossip . . .'

'You can't blame me for any gossip round the time of Anita Garner's disappearance. We're talking thirty years ago.'

'I didn't say *you*. I said people *like* you. Harry never laid a finger on Anita and we'd just about got to the point where everyone in Fethering had forgotten the accusation had even been made. Until you and your nosy neighbour started digging it all up again!'

'Just a minute, Veronica—'

'"Mrs Lasalle" to you!'

'Very well, Mrs Lasalle . . . are you sure that your husband committed suicide? Did he leave a note?'

'No, we haven't found any note. But that wouldn't have been Harry's way. He didn't come out with things. He kept it all bottled up inside. The way he died says quite as much as a note would have done.'

'What do you mean, exactly?'

'My husband virtually built *Harry's Dream* . . . well, built it up from an empty hull. He installed all the electrics, all the gas-powered stuff. He knew every inch of that boat. There's no way he would let the space fill with carbon monoxide *by accident*. No, Harry knew precisely what he was doing. He anchored out at sea, sabotaged the gas supply and drank a bottle of whisky to see him on his way. Harry knew what he was doing,' she repeated doggedly.

'If what you say is true—'

'Of course it's bloody true! Are you suggesting I didn't know my own husband?'

'No. All I'm saying is that, if he did commit suicide, are you sure the reason was the revival of all the allegations about him and Anita Garner?'

'What other reason could there be? If you're implying that there was something wrong with our marriage—'

'No, no, I'm certainly not. It's just . . . I only met your husband very briefly . . . at Fethering Yacht Club last Saturday . . . and I thought he seemed very depressed.'

'Oh? And what qualifications do you have to say whether someone's depressed or not?'

'I do have some experience of medical conditions. I work as a healer.'

'Huh.' Even Carole could hardly have bettered the level of scepticism in that 'Huh'.

'Your husband seemed to be depressed by his physical frailty, the fact that he couldn't go on working like he used to do.'

'Yes, all right. There were some adjustments he needed to make because of his age, but he'd have managed that all right. Harry wouldn't have been the first man to find the early stages of retirement difficult.'

'No, I agree. But he also seemed to be drinking a lot of whisky.'

'How much Harry drank was his business! He had a strong head for the booze. He was never out of control.'

'I'm not saying he was. He also talked that morning of not being able to go out in *Harry's Dream* for much longer. He talked of taking her out for one last trip.'

'All right.' Veronica Lasalle reacted as if her point had been proved. 'So that means he was already thinking about suicide, doesn't it?'

'It could do, yes. But his reasons for thinking about it might have been his increasing infirmity rather than anything to do with Anita Garner.'

'Well, it wasn't,' Veronica Lasalle asserted.

'He also' – Jude hazarded – 'seemed upset at the prospect of handing the business over to your son.'

This suggestion caused considerable annoyance. 'He wasn't handing the business over to our son! Roland has his own business. He's an architect and property developer. Harry was just a *builder*.' There was a lot of subtext in the way she said the word. It was clear that Veronica Lasalle had always considered she'd married beneath her.

She went on, 'Harry had nothing to do with the current development of Footscrow House into holiday flatlets. It's Roland's company that's doing that. Originally, Roly was going to employ Lasalle Build and Design on the project, but he found another builder who offered a better rate.'

'But wouldn't having his professional services rejected by his own son be just the kind of thing to turn Harry suicidal?'

'No. He was very proud of Roland's success. I made sure Roland had all the advantages his father hadn't. I never wanted him to be just a builder like Harry. I wanted my Roly to be a professional man – and that's what he is. Lives up in London and is working on projects all over the world. Footscrow House is small beer, by Roly's standards. He showed his father what real success looks like.'

Jude recognized in Veronica's words a whole rat's nest of potential family conflicts, but it wasn't the moment to explore them. Instead, she repeated, 'What we heard at Fethering Yacht Club gave me the impression that your husband was depressed by his increasing infirmity.'

'"We"? Who's this "we"?' the old woman asked sharply. 'Who were you with?'

'I was with Pete.'

'Oh well, you don't want to believe anything Pete says. He's a right little troublemaker.'

Strange. It was the first time Jude had heard anyone in Fethering say a word against the decorator. Except, of course, for Roland, who'd unjustly accused him of skiving at Footscrow House. What did the two surviving Lasalles have against Pete?

'I just think,' Jude reiterated, 'that your husband's reason for taking his own life might have been something other than those old allegations about him and Anita Garner.'

'You only say that because it lets you and your neighbour off the hook.'

'What do you mean?'

'I mean that Harry killed himself because that old accusation about him and Anita had resurfaced.'

'But—'

'And I blame you and Carole Seddon for his death!'

TEN

G uilt? Did Jude feel any guilt now? She had, after all, virtually been accused of murder.

But, for some reason, she didn't feel guilty. She tried to analyse why.

And decided that it was because she'd got such a clear impression of Veronica Lasalle having an agenda. Jude knew that bereavement affected people in different ways but she still found the woman's behaviour odd. Three days after hearing of the death of her husband of . . . what . . . forty years . . .? Given Roland's age, it might well be nearer fifty . . . Three days after hearing the devastating news of his death, Jude could believe the new widow might be full of anger and looking for someone to blame for the tragedy. Marching round to confront and bawl out the person she thought responsible did make a kind of sense.

But there were inconsistencies in how she'd behaved. For a start, though Veronica had demonstrated anger, she had not shown any signs of grief. Her main agenda seemed to have been to persuade Jude that Harry's death had been suicide. And that the reason why he had taken his own life was because of the return of long-buried allegations about his having had a sexual relationship with Anita Garner.

It could have been true. Veronica Lasalle was certainly determined that that explanation should be the accepted one.

Or had she been acting in that way simply to stop any other explanation being considered?

Jude didn't have long to mull over these thoughts because Pete soon returned. In fact, he returned so soon after Veronica's departure that he could have been waiting outside to watch her leave. What's more, his excuse about having to go to the trade counter didn't stack up. He had returned without any new paint.

Jude did not pass any comment on this. She just made him

another cup of coffee (white with one sugar). But, as she handed it across, Pete raised the subject himself.

'Sorry I had to leave. Veronica and me, we don't get on. Never have done.'

'Oh. Any reason?'

'Goes back a long way. She's a suspicious cow. Worked with Harry from way back, did all the paperwork when it was just plain "Lasalle Builders", long before it became "Lasalle Build and Design". And she always thought everyone was trying to rip them off.'

'Everyone including you?'

The decorator nodded. 'I was working for Brenton Wilkinson back then. Harry subcontracted him to do some decorating work on Footscrow House. And all the time we was there, Veronica kept her beady eyes on us, seeing we wasn't skiving.'

'Which, I can safely assume, you weren't?'

'No way. Well, I got rather sick of having her constantly on my case, so I played a trick on her. Something old Veronica has never forgiven me for.'

'"Trick"? What did you do?'

'Like I said, she constantly thought people were trying to get one over on her and, with the decorating, she thought we might be skimping the number of coats of paint we done. There are, I'm afraid, some chancers in the trade who *do* do that. You know, like, say in the care home bedrooms, the deal was we'd strip down the paintwork, windows and what-have-you, prime where necessary and put on two coats of gloss.

'Veronica, the suspicious cow, thought I was trying to get away with just doing the one and she'd try to catch me out. Overnight, when I'd left the first coat to dry, she'd sneak round with a pin and put a row of pinpricks in the paint . . . underside of a windowsill, somewhere like that, where nobody's likely to look, sort of place a skiving decorator might think they could get away with it. And then bloody Veronica'd check the next day to see her pinpricks had been covered by the second coat before she'd sign off on the job.

'Well, I don't like being distrusted – I suppose nobody does, really – so I hatched a little plan to catch her out. After she's checked her pinpricks was covered and signed the job off, I go back in the room with a pin of my own and put the holes back, through the second coat, exactly where they had been. Kept doing it. Drove Veronica bloody mad. Starts worrying whether she can believe the evidence of her own eyes.

'Mind you, pretty soon she works out it's me who's behind it. And I'm afraid, with someone like Veronica Lasalle, these things go deep. Our relationship – if we ever had one – hasn't been that harmonious ever since.'

'Yes, she was bad-mouthing you just now.'

'Was she? There's a surprise.'

'Which is unusual.'

'What?'

'Nobody in Fethering has a bad word to say about Pete the decorator.'

That prompted a reappearance of the toothy grin. 'Nice of you to say so.'

'When you were doing that job, Pete, you know, changing the care home into a boutique hotel, did you paint any of the bedrooms?'

'I don't think so. And it's so long ago, I can't remember what I did. So far as I recall, though, on that refurbishment most of the stuff I done was downstairs.'

'So, you hadn't been in that bedroom before, the one where we found the handbag?'

He shook his head. 'First time, that day we found it.'

'Are you Jude?'

She had just left the house, going to visit one of her regular clients who was virtually immobile but still managing to live on her own. Turning at the question, she saw it had come from Roland Lasalle. Except for his father's jutting lower jaw and underbite, his looks came more from his mother. He had her short stature and harsh features. His copper-beech-coloured hair was firmly slicked down with a clinically straight parting. He was wearing a dark mohair overcoat, the polish on his black shoes was lustrous, and he had just stepped out of an electric BMW. He must have been coming to Woodside Cottage to see her.

'Yes,' Jude acknowledged her name.

'My name's Roland Lasalle.' Of course, she knew that, but then again they hadn't had a proper Fethering introduction and, based in London, he might well not have registered seeing her before.

'Oh,' she said, before coming up with the appropriate formula: 'I was very sorry to hear about your father. I wish you—'

'Don't worry about that. I've just been talking to my mother.'

'Oh yes?'

'She's very upset.'

'I'm not surprised. With your father having just—'

'Not upset about that.' Realizing his words might have sounded inappropriate, he backtracked. 'Well, obviously she is. But more upset about what you've been doing.'

'Oh?'

'I was in London – that's where I'm based – and only came back down to Fethering when I heard about my father. So, I didn't know any of the stuff that's been going on.'

'What "stuff" do you mean?'

'My mother's only just told me about why people are suddenly talking about Anita Garner again.'

'Right.'

'That all seemed to have been forgotten – which was a great relief to my father, let me tell you. And then you bring the whole scandal back to life by finding the bloody girl's handbag!'

Jude was not going to stand for that. 'You make it sound like I deliberately went looking for the handbag. I just happened to be in the room when it was found.'

'With Pete the decorator.'

'Yes. And, in fact, I met you that day – or rather I saw you. You bawled out Pete for skiving.'

'Did I?' Roland Lasalle had no interest in their previous encounter. 'Pete's done worse than skiving. Don't know how he got that butter-wouldn't-melt-in-his-mouth image round Fethering.'

'I've heard no complaints about—'

'Anyway, *Jude*' – he managed to get a sneer into the name – 'you've done enough harm. My mother reckons you're the reason why my father topped himself. I don't know enough detail to support that accusation, but I do know that village gossip never did anyone any good. So, in future, will you and your neighbour keep your bloody mouths shut!'

With that, he got back into his electric BMW and slammed the door.

The care home was on the southern outskirts of Fedborough. Had it been the other side of the town, it would have commanded views over the South Downs. As it was, the building looked over the flatness of the coastal plain. The space between it and the English Channel was filled with endless rows of plastic tunnels for the growing of vegetables. But in the icy February drizzle, any outlook would have been dispiriting.

Nor was the interior of the home calculated to raise one's mood. There are, along the south of England's 'Costa Geriatrica', a wide range of accommodations for the elderly no longer able to look after themselves. Some have all the facilities of five-star hotels (with prices to match). Swimming pools, spas, gourmet cuisine, hairdressers, lectures, theatre visits, tours of National Trust properties, book clubs, bridge tournaments . . . all of these and more are available at the top end of the market. A first-class shuttle service to the grave.

Down in the local-authority-funded care homes, like the one Brenton Wilkinson was in, the amenities are more Spartan. Stripped-down budgets and shortage of staff meant there wasn't much spare capacity to do anything beyond the basics of getting the residents out of bed, feeding them and getting them back into bed at the (early) end of the day. The air was flavoured by the competing smells of urine and disinfectant.

In terms of mental stimulation, there was a library of dog-eared books, whose print was too small for most of the inmates to read, some incomplete boxes of board games and decks of cards.

For most, the only entertainment on offer was daytime television, played at far too high a volume in the day room. Most visitors to the residents had to conduct their conversations, however intimate the subject matter might be, against that background.

Malk Penberthy had arranged the visit to Brenton Wilkinson and he accompanied Carole. Seeing the two men together and knowing them to be contemporaries, Carole was struck by how much better the journalist had worn than the decorator. Probably something to do with what Jude had reported from her conversation with Pete, about the physical strains of a whole lifetime of manual labour. The life of the mind brought its own challenges, but not the same bodily stresses.

Brenton Wilkinson was huge, spilling out of the threadbare armchair into which he had been propped. Presumably, during his working life, much of his bulk had been muscle, but spending all day watching stupid people answering stupid quiz questions, and marginally less stupid people trying to make money from auctions, had turned it all to fat. There was no hair visible on his head; his face and hands were blotched with dark brown liver spots. His lips were sucked in. When he opened his mouth not a single tooth was visible.

No teeth maybe, but Brenton Wilkinson appeared to have all his marbles intact. Forewarned of their visitation, he greeted Carole by name before Malk had a chance to introduce them.

It wasn't the easiest place to conduct any kind of conversation. But the care home had no quieter rooms available, and visitors were only allowed in the bedrooms if the resident was unwell and confined to bed.

To one side of Brenton Wilkinson sat a frail old woman with wispy white hair who kept, every couple of minutes, saying with what sounded like satisfaction, 'Oh no, he won't.'

On the other side, an equally frail old woman was knitting a square of green wool. Soon after Carole and Malk's arrival, she completed the job, then unravelled it, wound up the wool into a ball, cast on and started knitting the square all over again.

'Carole,' Malk Penberthy managed to make himself heard over the television hubbub, 'was interested in the decorating you did back at Footscrow House.'

'"Footscrow House"?' The old decorator let out a wheezy, liquid chuckle. '"Fiasco House" more likely. That place has a . . . what's that thing young people say? A "death kiss" about it?'

'"A kiss of death" . . .?' Carole suggested tentatively, trying not to sound as if she were correcting him.

She needn't have worried. 'Yes, "kiss of death"!' he echoed cheerily. 'God, the money I made out of Fiasco House over the years . . . Every time the latest company owning it goes bust, the new one wants it all redecorated. And fortunately, I've got a good name round Fethering, so I keep getting recommended and end up doing the job. The number of layers of paint me and my boys have put on that building doesn't bear thinking of. Footscrow House was my Forth Bridge, you know. I done very nicely out of it.'

'I'm glad to hear it,' said Carole. 'I wonder—?'

But before she could ask another, more specific question, Brenton was away again. 'Coo, hard work it was back then. Today's decorators don't know they're born. It's all easy for them.'

'In what way?' asked Carole, careful not to put the old man off by rushing him.

'Well, a lot of it's technology, new inventions and stuff. When I started, way back when, we didn't have any rollers, for one thing. Done everything with brushes, haven't we? And all the ladders was made of wood. Heavy to pull those buggers around – pardon my French. Easy with the aluminium ones they've got now.

'And the paint – blimey, the technology's changed there. Some of it we had to mix up ourselves. Snowcem for exterior masonry . . . well, that's still a powder. But the mixing for the colours – we had to do a bit of that when I started out. And working with thinners and driers and I don't know what else. Lot simpler once they got vinyl into paints. Easy with colours now, too. You just go down your local trade counter and buy your paint all mixed up and ready to go.'

The sentence ended in a bout of coughing. Again, Carole thought she might get in with a question, but Brenton recovered too quickly and continued, 'Of course, the big change come in the 1970s and 80s – that's when you get some of the one-coat paints being developed. And then, non-drip comes in then, and all. Blimey, that makes a difference! Yeah, you still need to put sheets over the furniture, and that, but when you're doing a ceiling, you don't get your overalls all splattered like you used to.

'We done ceilings with six-inch brushes in my day. Hamilton Perfection was the best brushes. Still are. Cost more but last longer. Mind you, back then you had to spend a long time cleaning the ceilings before you could start on the painting. Nicotine, particularly if you was doing a pub or somewhere like that. God, it was a messy business. Today's kids may call themselves decorators, but they don't know the half of it.'

The chuckle that followed this developed into a more serious spasm of coughing. Clearly, a lifetime of breathing in paint fumes, and who could say what else, hadn't done much good for the old boy's respiratory system.

As the coughing subsided, Carole did manage to get a question in. 'Do you remember when you did the decorating after Harry Lasalle changed Footscrow House from being a care home to a boutique hotel?'

'Certainly do,' said Brenton Wilkinson. 'And I bet I know why you're asking.'

'Oh?'

'Because that was around the time that Anita Garner disappeared, wasn't it?'

'It was.'

'Oh yes, I remember that well. The police were very keen to talk to me and my lads about that. Well, they reckoned the fact that we were outsiders made us suspicious. Everyone else in the building had been working there for a while. We'd only just been brought in to do the decorating. And a couple of the lads hadn't been working for me that long. I didn't know what they'd done in the past . . . well, only the bits they chose to tell me. So, we went through quite a lot of questioning.'

But, if Carole thought she was about to get the detail she wanted, she was in for a disappointment, as Brenton Wilkinson went off on another tangent. 'One of the lads was still doing his apprenticeship. Four days a week working with me, one day in college. We all done apprenticeships back then, that was the way it worked. Mind you, there was no college when I started, just working for a right difficult old bugger – pardon my French. He kept my nose to the grindstone, all right.

'And when we was apprentices then, we had to drink a pint of milk every day before we started work. It was the lead in the paint, you see. Milk supposed to line your stomach, so's it didn't poison you.' He wheezed. 'Mind you, I think it was the asbestos in some of the schools we painted that did for me.'

'I'm sorry,' said Carole, leaping in as he paused for another gulp of air. 'What did the police actually ask you about the—?'

But he hadn't finished talking about apprenticeships. 'Do you know what the lads did on their college days? Oh, they had

lectures and stuff, but they also each had their little station, a bit
of wall with a door in it. They had to wallpaper it, paint the door
and the architraves, all the right primers, right number of coats,
all that. Minute they'd finished it and had it inspected and marked
– tough taskmasters they had then – they have to strip off the
wallpaper, remove the paint, sand down the surfaces, get them
back to being totally undecorated. Soon as they've done that,
they have to start again, wallpapering, priming, all the right coats
of primer and paint. And they keep doing that one day a week
for four years. God knows how many times they did the full
sequence. But tell you what – those lads certainly knew how to
decorate a doorway!'

The high note on which Brenton finished this speech set off
a really serious attack of coughing. What he'd said about asbestos
had Carole really worried. She looked around the crowded room
for a carer but there was none in sight. She exchanged an anxious
look with Malk Penberthy who said, 'I'll go and get him a glass
of water.'

By the time Malk came back, Brenton Wilkinson's coughing
had subsided into rasping breaths that shuddered through his
body. He looked totally exhausted by the spasm. His visitors
realized they couldn't stay much longer. Selfishly, Carole hoped
he'd still be able to give her the information she sought.

The old decorator took a long swig of water and was silent
for a moment.

'Oh no, he won't,' chuckled the woman beside him, for the
umpteenth time. The woman on the other side was once again
unravelling her square of green wool.

'Are you all right to talk?' asked Carole.

All the huge body seemed to shake as he nodded.

'I just wondered, when the police talked to you, you know,
when they were investigating Anita Garner's disappearance, what
kind of questions did they ask?'

'Well, it wasn't me so much they talked to. I wasn't there on
the day she vanished. I was busy down at a school we was
repainting. The Footscrow House job was one of ours, right, but
it was the lads who was doing the actual decorating there. So, it
was mostly them they talked to.'

'And do you know what kind of things they asked?'

'Oh, usual kind of stuff. If any of them had taken a shine to Anita. If they'd come on to her. If they'd seen anyone else come on to her. If they'd seen anything suspicious.'

'Had they?'

'None of them told if they had. So, eventually, the cops gave up talking to them.'

'And did any of your lads talk to you about Anita Garner?'

'Nothing important. She was a nice-looking kid, though. And they was young boys, always got their eyes out for a pretty bit of skirt – oh, I'm probably not allowed to say that now, am I? Not *politically correct*.' He put his idea of a precious accent on the last two words.

'Don't worry about that. But one of your apprentices did say he fancied Anita?'

'Well, yes. But it was just, like, you know, banter.'

'What did he say?'

'Just he reckoned she was a bit of all right.'

'And what was his name?'

'Pete. You probably know him. Everyone in Fethering knows Pete.'

'Yes, I know him,' said Carole. 'Did he reckon a lot of women were "a bit of all right"?'

'Yeah. Back then. He was just a kid, like I said. Had an eye for the ladies, like most lads that age. Pete's all settled down with wife and kiddies now. Has been for years.'

'Hm.' Carole nodded thoughtfully. 'And was he there, at Footscrow House, decorating, on the last day Anita Garner was seen?'

'He would have been, yes. Unless it was a Thursday. That was his college day, stripping down and repainting his blooming doorway.'

'The last day Anita Garner was seen,' said Malk Penberthy with great precision, 'was a Tuesday.'

'And where in Footscrow House would Pete have been working?' asked Carole.

'Upstairs,' said Brenton Wilkinson. 'Pete was in charge of doing the bedrooms.'

ELEVEN

Seeing the decorator's van outside Woodside Cottage, as soon as she got back to High Tor Carole phoned her neighbour and asked her round for a cup of coffee.

They quickly brought each other up to date. Jude could not suppress a level of shock at the fact that Pete seemed to have lied to her. An uncomfortable feeling about him had been building up for a while, and now she seemed to have confirmation of her worst fears.

Jude also realized that she hadn't seen Carole since her visit to Glen Porter's beach hut and gave her the edited highlights of that encounter.

'And you're sure he and Lauren Givens are having an affair?'

'There are certain unmistakable signs.'

'Oh well, of course,' said Carole sniffily, 'you'd know more about that than I would.' Jude was far too canny to rise to the implied insult, so her neighbour went on, 'Of course, people having affairs are taking big risks.'

'Sorry?'

'Exposing themselves to danger.'

'Still not with you.'

'Well, it's obvious. Someone who's having an affair wants to keep it secret.'

Jude could actually think of quite a few acquaintances who wanted to shout about their affairs from the rooftops, but she didn't take issue. She knew it wouldn't be worth the effort. Just wait and see where her neighbour was going with this.

'So,' Carole continued her logic through, 'people having affairs put themselves at risk of exposure.'

'Blackmail?'

'Possibly even that. But news of an affair reaching the betrayed spouse can have pretty devastating effects too.'

'What are you saying, Carole?'

'I am saying that if, as you insist – on, it has to be said, very little evidence – that Glen Porter and Lauren Givens are having an affair, they might be prepared to go to great lengths to keep it a secret.'

'All right. I'll go along with that. So . . .?'

'You know Lauren . . .'

'Not very well.'

'Have you seen anyone threatening her?'

'Carole, I hardly know the woman. Where would I have seen anyone threatening her?'

But even as she said the words, a little scene she had observed came back to Jude. Fethering Yacht Club, Harry Lasalle on his way out, being accosted by Lauren Givens. Her asking him for something. Him turning her down and leaving the bar.

It could have meant anything. It could have meant nothing. On the other hand, that Saturday had turned out to be the last day of Harry Lasalle's life. Surely, anything that happens to someone on the last day of their life takes on a special relevance?

'It might be interesting to talk to her,' Jude conceded.

'And we have the perfect opportunity to do just that,' said Carole triumphantly. 'The timing is perfect. Today is Wednesday.'

She brandished a flyer picked up off the kitchen table.

'Fancy going to a Pottery Open Day?'

Neither Carole nor Jude would claim to be an *aficionado* when it came to ceramic toadstools. Jude had never felt the lack of one in her life and Carole was of the view that they were common, the interior décor version of garden gnomes. And 'common' was one of the worst words in Carole Seddon's lexicon.

Neither of them had been to the Givens's house before but, like most places in the village, it was within walking distance. In De Vere Road, an upmarket address in Fethering. All of the houses there had at least five bedrooms and substantial gardens. The owners thought De Vere Road was the best place to live in the village – or possibly the world. In this opinion, they were constantly challenged by people who lived on the Shorelands Estate, who were of the view that their seaside location gave them the edge. Basically, the issue was one of money. Residents of the one location were desperate to assert that they had more money than residents of the other location. That was how life worked at the upmarket end of Fethering.

There was a neatly printed notice attached to the gatepost, which read: 'POTTERY OPEN DAY'. An arrow directed visitors towards the 'STUDIO', a kind of conservatory attached to the side of the main building. It had a separate entrance which was crested by another printed notice, again reading: 'STUDIO'. In spite of the cold weather, the door to this was open, though a thick red velvet curtain was hung across the inside as a draught excluder.

There was no bell or knocker in evidence, so Carole and Jude pushed their way through. The studio was very tidy and well-appointed. No expense had been spared. The kiln and other equipment looked to be new and state-of-the-art. The interior was highly heated and the condensation on the inside of the windows gave the feeling of a greenhouse.

But there were no plants on display. Nor were there any other people inside inspecting what was on offer. The idea of a Pottery Open Day in a village like Fethering might be just about viable in the summer. A few punters, day-trippers and holidaymakers might amble in then. But in a particularly cold February? There weren't that many art-lovers in Fethering. If you excluded those who didn't regard ceramic toadstools as up there with Leonardo and Michelangelo, there were even fewer. And the number of those who fancied going out on a cold Wednesday morning . . . No surprise, really, that Lauren Givens wasn't fighting off the crowds.

Not only was the studio empty of other visitors, it was also empty of the artist, or craftswoman, or ceramicist, whose artefacts were on display. Small notices on the shelves not only indicated which area of the ceramic toadstool world each section repre-sented, but also their prices.

Carole and Jude moved silently along, scanning the exhibits. The former was appalled by what was on offer. She felt sure that, for some people, ceramic toadstools were . . . a word she even winced to think of . . . 'collectibles'. But, for her, the differ-ence between a Red Polka Dot ceramic toadstool and a Magic Fairy ceramic toadstool was not of importance in the Great Scheme of Things.

She did, however, see one selection that made her nudge Jude and point. The sign read: 'TINKLING TOADSTOOLS'. These were tall, with pointy ends like partially opened umbrellas, painted, like all the other artefacts, in garishly bright colours. And, presumably, if touched, they would tinkle.

Carole was about to put this function to the test, when Jude's hand on her arm stopped her. A voice could be heard coming through the open door to the kitchen in the main house.

It was Fred Givens. There was a note of irritation as he asked, 'Lauren, have you checked if there's anyone out there?'

'Of course I haven't!' There was more than a note of irritation in her reply. 'There's no point in looking every five minutes, when the chances are nobody's going to come all bloody day!'

'People will come. That is, they will if you got enough flyers out there. It was a bloody good flyer. I got one of my top designers to do it. The trouble is, Lauren, you have no understanding of the basic principles of marketing.'

'Fred, will you get off my case! I know enough about marketing to know how many of my ceramic toadstools I can sell. I go back to the same gift shops every quarter and they order more or less exactly the same number of items. And that works for me.'

'Yes, but a business shouldn't be static. It needs to keep expanding. It's like that Woody Allen line about relationships. "A relationship's like a shark. It has to constantly move forward or it dies." Businesses are like that, too.'

'Not just businesses,' Lauren muttered.

'What? What do you mean?'

'I mean, Fred, it's a while since our relationship moved forward, wouldn't you say?'

'No. We've been fine for—'

'Not true, Fred. We haven't been fine for years. And all this time you've been "working from home", it's got less fine by the minute.'

'I thought you liked having me around.' He sounded aggrieved and a little pathetic.

'I don't like having you *constantly* around. Interfering all the time.'

'Interfering?'

'Yes, like this bloody Pottery Open Day. I never wanted a Pottery Open Day. And it's now pretty damn clear that nobody in Fethering wants a Pottery Open Day either. But you kept bloody insisting I should do it.'

'Lauren . . . darling . . . I'm trying to help you. As you've just admitted, you have no experience of marketing. I've spent an entire career in the business. And I'm just sharing some of my skills with you. Most wives would be delighted to have their husband putting a gentle hand on the tiller of their business.'

'Well then, I am clearly not "most wives"! I don't want "a gentle hand on the tiller of my business"! I want you to mind your own bloody business!'

'Lauren,' said Fred, 'that's very hurtful.'

'So? Maybe I want to bloody hurt you.'

'But why would you want to do that?'

'God, you're so dense sometimes!'

There was a silence. Carole and Jude, who'd been breathlessly quiet during their eavesdropping, exchanged looks. Was Lauren about to come into the studio? Should they make a noise and pretend they'd only just arrived? Or should they sneak out on tiptoe?

'Lauren . . .' Fred began tentatively.

His reward was a testy, 'What?'

'Is it true . . . what Harry Lasalle said?'

'What did Harry Lasalle say?'

'Oh, come on, you can't have forgotten. We discussed it at the time.'

'I don't remember,' said Lauren dismissively.

'He said that . . . He was just passing on gossip, but Harry'd heard rumours that you'd been secretly seeing Glen Porter and—'

'Oh, for God's sake, Fred!'

There was a sudden screech of a chair being pushed back on a stone floor. Carole and Jude looked at each other in alarm. But Lauren didn't come out to the studio. Instead, they heard the slamming of an internal door. She had stormed out of the kitchen into the rest of the house.

Carole and Jude exchanged looks of agreement. Then they tiptoed out into De Vere Road.

Both sharing the same thought: that neither Fred nor Lauren Givens had intended their Pottery Open Day to be quite that open.

There were other shared thoughts going through their minds as they walked back to the High Street.

'If,' said Carole meditatively, 'we were to take the view that Harry Lasalle knew about the supposed affair between Lauren Givens and Glen Porter . . .'

'It's not a "supposed affair",' Jude objected. 'It's an actual affair.'

'We have no proof of that. You surmised there was something going on . . .'

'It's more than "surmised", Carole. I *know* there's something going on. And, for heaven's sake – given what we've just heard Fred Givens say . . .'

'Lauren didn't allow him the opportunity to say much. She stormed out of the room.'

'Yes, but it was clear that they'd talked about the subject before.'

'Maybe,' said Carole. 'All right, let's say for a moment that what you're suggesting is true.'

'It is!' Jude protested.

'*If* it is, then, going back to what I was saying earlier about the security risk involved in having affairs . . .'

'Yes,' said Jude patiently.

'. . . and if Harry Lasalle knew what was going on and threatened to spill the beans . . .'

'Which I'm pretty sure he did.' Jude told Carole about the scene she'd witnessed between Harry and Lauren at Fethering Yacht Club. 'Suppose he'd threatened to make what he knew about the affair public and Lauren had been trying to persuade him not to . . .'

'If that were true,' said Carole, 'then we have a whole new range of motivations for people to want him dead.'

'Assuming he didn't kill himself.'

'Do you honestly think he did?'

'I really don't know.' Jude grimaced. 'What I do know, though, is that both his mother and son are convinced he did.'

'Or possibly,' suggested Carole, 'they, for reasons of their own, want everyone else to be convinced he did.'

'You could be right.'

'So, where do we go next with our investigation? We're still working on the assumption that the two crimes – Anita Garner's disappearance and Harry Lasalle's death – are connected?'

'Yes, we are,' said Jude doggedly.

'So, I say again, what do we do next? What lead do we follow up?'

Jude's face took on a look of determination. 'I'd like to find out, one way or the other, whether there's any justification for being suspicious of Pete.'

Coffee back at High Tor. Jude didn't want to face the decorator again until she'd sorted a few details out in her mind.

Carole supplied the drinks and they sat in the kitchen. From in front of the Aga, Gulliver's snores rumbled peaceably in the background.

'I don't want to harp on about adultery,' said Carole, 'but if Harry Lasalle did know about what was going on between Lauren Givens and Glen Porter . . .'

'Yes,' Jude completed, 'that might, in some rather far-fetched scenario, give either of them a motive to kill him.'

'Not that" far-fetched". Adultery,' Carole insisted, with the confidence of someone who'd had no experience of it, 'can stir strong emotions.'

'Undoubtedly,' agreed Jude, who did have some experience of it, from both sides of the blanket, as wife and mistress. 'But at the moment, I'm more interested in Pete.'

'In connection with what?' asked Carole. 'Anita Garner's disappearance? Or Harry Lasalle's death?'

'Either. Or both,' Jude replied vaguely. There was some relevant detail somewhere in the depths of her mind which she was having difficulty bringing to the surface.

'Well,' said Carole logically, 'why don't you analyse the basis for your suspicion of Pete, the Paragon of Fethering?'

'It's things other people have said. There is clearly bad blood between him and Veronica Lasalle. He couldn't stand being in the same room as her. And she described him as "a right little troublemaker". Not the image most people in Fethering have of him.'

'No, but Veronica has just lost her husband. She must be in a state of shock. Maybe she wasn't thinking straight.'

'Hm.' The reference to Pete's image reminded Jude of Roland Lasalle's words: 'Pete's done worse than skiving.' She relayed them to Carole.

'The Lasalle family certainly seem to have it in for him.'

'But Harry was perfectly friendly last Saturday at the yacht club.'

'Yes. I've no idea what's going on there.' Carole looked thoughtful. 'And then, of course, there's what Brenton Wilkinson told me . . . about Pete thinking Anita was "a bit of all right".'

'Mm. That worried me when you told me. Mind you, it was a long time ago. He was only a boy. And there's a long history of young men fancying young women. No, the thing that worries me most is Pete actually lying to me.'

'About the rooms he was painting at Footscrow House when Anita Garner disappeared?'

'Exactly. Pete told me he was working downstairs, but you say Brenton Wilkinson said he was working upstairs.'

'He was very firm about that.'

'And also, Pete swore blind he'd never before been in the room where we found Anita Garner's handbag.'

Carole's lips pursed with suspicion.

'But, Carole, why would Pete lie?'

'Hiding something?'

'Yes, that's the usual explanation, isn't it? To put me off the scent. But what scent?'

'Also,' Carole continued deploying her logic, 'if Pete knew that Anita Garner's handbag was hidden behind that panel, why on earth would he open it up with you there as a witness?'

Jude shook her head. She had no answer to that question either. And she wasn't enjoying being suspicious of Pete.

With a positive effort, she redirected her thoughts. Glen Porter . . . There was something Glen Porter had said when she saw him at his beach hut *dacha*. What was it? Was that the elusive memory that was nagging at her?

'I was just thinking,' she said, piecing it together, 'I told you what Glen Porter said when I went to see him . . .'

'Yes.'

'He was talking about you and me "digging into things" which didn't concern us.'

'Huh.' Carole Seddon's Home Office soul was offended. 'We're only behaving in the way any public-spirited person should behave.'

Jude wasn't entirely convinced by that, but she let it go. 'And Glen said that our investigations were likely to cause pain to someone . . . to some woman.'

'If wrongdoing has occurred,' Carole insisted stoutly, 'then inevitably revealing it is going to cause pain to someone.'

'Maybe. Anyway, when he was talking, I thought it was about Anita Garner . . . that she – or more likely her surviving friends and relations – might be hurt by having the whole story dug up again . . .'

'Mm?'

'But now, given what we know about Glen and Lauren, I wonder if it was *her* he was worrying about getting hurt.'

'Which would mean, Jude, that he thought we already knew about the affair . . .'

'Yes.'

'Which we certainly didn't at that point.'

'No.'

'So,' said Carole slowly, 'where would he have got that idea from?'

'Guilty conscience?'

'Glen's certainly feeling guilty about something.' Jude rubbed her chin thoughtfully. 'I wonder what it is . . .?'

Jude felt awkward about being faced with Pete when she got back to Woodside Cottage, but she needn't have worried. There was a note propped up on the mantelpiece of her sitting room. 'HAD TO LEAVE THE GLOSS TO DRY. A BIT OF TIDYING-UP NEXT TWO DAYS, THEN WE'LL BE DONE. ALL THE BEST, PETE'.

He'd said he'd finish within the week. And the next day was Thursday. Pete was being true to his word. If only she could be certain he was true to his word in all areas of his life.

TWELVE

Jude's phone rang about half past five that afternoon. It was a rather secretive and excited-sounding Vi Benyon.

'Listen, Jude, Leslie's away. He's visiting his sister in Aberystwyth.'

'Oh.' This sounded like a bit of gratuitous information.

But its relevance soon became clear. 'And, the thing is, Jude, that means I can talk more freely. Leslie's a wonderful man but there are some things he doesn't like me to talk about.'

'Things you want to talk about?'

'Yes.'

Jude didn't just believe in synchronicity. She believed in other divine forces, possibly even a God. But she didn't believe in coincidence. When, apparently fortuitously, things worked out, they were meant to work out. And, at that moment, they seemed to be working out wonderfully.

'I was very shocked,' said Vi Benyon, 'to hear about Harry Lasalle's death.'

'I'm sure we all were.'

'And it got me thinking about all that Anita Garner business again.'

'Me too.'

'So, I wondered if we could meet and talk about it . . .? You sounded very interested when we were in the Crown and Anchor last week.'

Jude couldn't believe how serendipitously things were turning out.

'Yes, I was very interested. Well, still am very interested.'

'And, you see, Jude, with Leslie being away, as I say, I could talk about things more freely.'

'That would be wonderful.'

'So . . . what? Back in the Crown and Anchor?'

'Perfect. Do you mind if my neighbour Carole comes along too?'

'No. She was as interested as you were, wasn't she?'
'You can say that again.'

Mercifully, when Carole and Jude got to the Crown and Anchor
round six, Barney Poulton was not present. Maybe his wife had
dragged him back to the bridge table. Maybe it was the only way
she knew of shutting him up.

In fact, apart from Ted Crisp behind the bar, there was only
one other customer. Sitting demurely on a stool the customer
side was, much to Carole's annoyance, Brandie Neville.

She greeted Jude with a fulsome hug. About to offer the same
to Carole, the potential recipient's body language decided her
against the idea. She sat back on her stool. The landlord looked
at her soupily.

'Have you been using your precious gift today, Jude?' asked
Brandie.

'What, you mean healing? No, I'm having my treatment room
decorated.'

'"Treatment room"?' Carole couldn't stop herself from
echoing. 'You mean "sitting room".'

Jude grinned easily. 'Whatever.'

'It is not the name of the room that matters,' said Brandie. 'It
is the power that emanates from it.'

'Yes, that's so true.' Carole couldn't believe it – the words
had come from Ted Crisp.

And he went on, 'I may have been dismissive of the power
of healing in the past but—'

'"Dismissive"?' said Carole. 'One of your descriptions of it I
remember was "a load of old cobblers".'

'Ah well,' said Ted awkwardly. 'One can be wrong about
things.'

'The truth is always out there,' said Brandie. 'And it will be
there whenever a person comes to it.'

Carole seethed inwardly. Was every pronouncement of
Brandie's going to take the form of a gift-shop motto? Maybe
Lauren Givens could start printing them on ceramic toadstools
. . .? There'd undoubtedly be a market for them. There were, in
Carole's view, enough stupid people out in the world to buy any
old rubbish.

'You're so right, Brandie,' said Ted. 'So many of us go through life, seeing only the surface of things, totally unaware of their spiritual dimension.'

Carole caught Jude's eye and saw that her neighbour was having difficulty suppressing giggles. Though she treated her healing with great seriousness, and might share comparable thoughts with like-minded friends, she could recognize how incongruous they sounded coming out of the previously unreconstructed mouth of Ted Crisp.

Brandie smiled serenely. 'That's it, lovie.'

'Lovie'! Carole's mind echoed in appalled silence.

'I've been introducing Ted to mindfulness,' Brandie continued. 'Haven't I, lovie?'

'Yes, lovie. I'm not quite there yet,' the landlord admitted. 'I'm getting myself better at living in the moment, you know, being aware of the present, but my mind does keep wandering to the past and the future.'

'Early days,' said Brandie. 'You'll get better at it, lovie.'

'Yes.' Ted looked earnestly at Jude. 'I'm trying to learn mindfulness and meditation kind of . . . hand-in-glove.'

'Often the best way,' she reassured him.

'And I'm learning to repeat a tantra.'

'Mantra, lovie,' Brandie corrected gently.

'Yeah, right. I keep getting those two mixed up.'

'You'll catch on quickly,' said Brandie, 'if you just hang loose and let your thoughts flow free.'

The imminent implosion of Carole Seddon's brain was prevented by the arrival in the Crown and Anchor of Vi Benyon.

Vi without Leslie Benyon was a revelation. She'd been garrulous on their previous encounter in the Crown and Anchor but, Carole and Jude realized now, she had only been going at half-speed. Without her husband's restraining presence, she was a real motor-mouth. And she seemed to gain energy from being the centre of attention.

That was not the only change. When Carole offered her a drink, rather than the modest half-pint she'd made last for the whole of her previous visit, she asked for a large Scotch 'with some ice, no water'.

Once the three of them were ensconced in one of the bar's alcoves (mercifully out of earshot of spiritual endearments from the two 'lovies' at the bar), Vi started talking. In a way that suggested she had no intention of stopping.

'I wanted to contact you two as soon as I heard about Harry Lasalle's death. Terrible business. And in his own boat. *Harry's Dream.* He loved that boat, built it up from just a shell, you know. And he knew it inside out. I can't see him dying by accident in a boat he'd designed and built himself.'

'No,' said Jude.

'There's been talk round Fethering – heard it from one of my neighbours in Allinstore' – the village's uniquely inefficient supermarket – 'that Harry topped himself.'

'That's certainly what his family seem to believe.'

'Oh?'

Jude told Vi what she'd heard from Veronica and Roland Lasalle. 'And when we last spoke on the phone, you were about to tell me who came on to Anita Garner in Footscrow House. Was it Harry?'

The old lady nodded. 'That was the rumour I heard. As I say, I was so caught up with Mum's final illness that I didn't have much time to think about it, but that's what people were saying.'

'Veronica Lasalle came to see me . . .' said Jude.

'Lucky you. I'm sure she found something to bawl you out about.'

'Certainly did. She accused Carole and me of driving her husband to suicide.'

'Oh. Well. I suppose that's quite a major accusation. But she would have found something else if she hadn't had that. Veronica's one of those women who can always find fault with everyone.'

'But what she did tell me,' said Jude, 'was that Harry couldn't have come on to Anita at Footscrow House because she was there. She, Veronica, was running the care home with her husband, so he couldn't have got up to any hanky-panky with her there.'

'Huh.' Vi Benyon wasn't persuaded by that. 'Then she underestimated the deviousness of men . . . or particularly the deviousness of Harry Lasalle.'

'Are you suggesting,' asked Carole, 'that he had a bit of a reputation for coming on to members of his staff?'

'Yes, he did. But, of course, coming on to Anita Garner was especially cruel.'

'Oh? Why?'

'As I say, I heard a lot about Anita from my mum. They talked a lot, you know, during the last months. And the thing Mum kept saying to me was how young Anita was. Not young in age but young in experience. Wide-eyed and innocent. What's that French word beginning with "n"?'

'"Naïve"?' Jude suggested.

'That's the one. "Naïve" – that's what Anita was. Partly it was the Catholic thing. Her dad was very strict about all that stuff. Old-fashioned, like someone from fifty years before. If Anita had told him that she was having sex before marriage, or having an affair, he would have literally turned her out of the house. That's why I said, if Harry was coming on to her – and the general view seemed to be that he was – it would have been very cruel.'

'So,' asked Carole, 'Harry had always had a reputation for that kind of thing?'

'I think it got worse as Roland got older. Happens with some men. They see their son working his way through girlfriends, without a care in the world, and they get kind of antsy, stuck with the original – and, it has to be said, ageing – wife. Basic jealousy. I know Leslie got a bit strange when Kent started having girlfriends.' She chuckled throatily. 'I had to use all my feminine wiles to make him realize nothing out there was as good as what he'd got at home.'

Carole and Jude joined in the chuckles. Neither had expected quite such frankness.

'I believe,' said Carole, quoting some survey that she'd once read in a colour supplement, 'that men – and women – who'd grown up before the pill was available got very jealous of the sexual freedom enjoyed by their children's generation.'

'I'm sure they did,' said Vi, 'but I hope you're not including me in that category.'

'Sorry?'

'I'm not that old. The pill was certainly around when I got to my teens. And I took full advantage of it. Let me tell you, there were a good few – very enjoyable – dry runs before I ended up tying the knot with Leslie.'

Jude grinned. Carole looked slightly shocked. Both reflected on how easy it is to write off the old and treat them as if they were always that age, showing no interest in the people they had been before. Vi Benyon hadn't always looked like a cottage loaf. In her time, she had clearly been something of a little raver.

Jude had a thought – a long shot but worth asking. 'Vi, going off at a complete tangent, do you remember which room your mother was in while she was at Footscrow House?'

'Of course I do. I spent enough time visiting her there.'

'Was it at the front of the building or the back?'

'Front. Nice sea view. Mum appreciated that. She knew she was on the way out and kept saying how grateful she was that she'd go with the sight of the sea in her eyes. She enjoyed the whiff of salt and seaweed. Had always lived by the sea, always in Fethering.'

'Could you describe exactly where the room was?'

Carole caught on to what her neighbour was doing and listened intently as Vi fixed the precise location of her mother's last residence. 'Of course, they was tiny little compartments. Big rooms divided up with partitions to fit in as many paying customers as possible. Not much better than rabbit hutches, really.'

'And, in your mother's room,' asked Jude excitedly, 'was there a sort of triangular alcove that had been boarded over?'

She was due for a disappointment. 'No,' said Vi Benyon firmly. 'The room was just a rectangle, a bit of it partitioned off for the bathroom, of course. No secret compartments or odd bits sticking out anywhere.'

'Oh,' said Jude flatly. Carole looked equally deflated.

'Mind you,' said Vi, 'your alcove could have been in the room next door.'

'Did you know the resident who had that room?' asked Carole. The moment she'd said it, she realized it was a rather useless question. They were talking about thirty years before. And the basic reason why people go to a care home is to die. They weren't going to find any useful witnesses still extant.

But Vi Benyon's reply was more helpful than she'd expected. 'That room didn't have any residents in it. It was a staff bedroom. You know, if one of the carers had to stay overnight, that's where they'd go.'

'Did you ever go into the room?'

'No, Jude. It was always locked. And visitors weren't encouraged to go wandering round other residents' rooms, anyway.'

'Did you ever hear people inside the room?'

'No. Well, I wouldn't have done. It was a bedroom for overnight stays, and I was always visiting Mum during the daytime . . . until the very end, that is.'

'And the room was narrow?' asked Jude.

'I told you. They all were. Like rabbit hutches.'

Carole could tell, from Jude's expression, that these questions had a logical relevance for her. Frustratingly, she could also tell that the explanation wouldn't come until the two of them were alone together.

But the momentary silence gave Carole an opportunity to redirect the investigation down a path of her choosing. 'The other person, we've heard rumours, who might have had more than friendly designs on Anita Garner was Glen Porter. You say your son Kent was at school with him . . .?'

'Yes.'

'And Glen was popular with the girls?'

'Popular at first. They couldn't get enough of him. Less popular when he dumped them.'

'Ah. And you think Anita might have been one of his conquests?'

'According to Kent, Glen claimed she was. But I'm not so sure.'

'Why not?'

'Because of what I've just talked about. The Catholic thing. Fear of her dad. I'm sure a lot of the girls at school would have fallen for Glen Porter's rather obvious charms. I'm not sure that Anita Garner would have done, though.'

'But, according to Kent, Glen claimed to have seduced her?'

'Kent didn't actually put it in those words. Glen more "implied" than actually "claimed". With boys round that age, there's a lot of big talk, claiming they've had sex with lots of girls they've never been near.'

'So, you don't think Glen Porter did have sex with Anita Garner?'

'I'd be surprised, because of the kind of girl I knew she

was. Afraid of her father's reaction, like I said. But a Jack-the-Lad like Glen would make all kinds of claims. Boys of that age can be very cruel. Say nasty things about girls which the girls themselves can't deny. All kinds of rubbish. And I gather it's worse now with all this social media they've got. Sending compromising photos to all and sundry – horrible. Thank God I'm too old to have anything to do with Facebook and Witter.'

Neither of the women corrected her. In fact, both thought the malapropism was rather appropriate.

Jude went off on another tangent. 'Did your mother ever hear Anita mention a Spanish boyfriend called Pablo?'

'No. Anita never mentioned any boyfriends to her.'

Carole offered more drinks. Vi was happy to accept another large Scotch. Jude didn't have to spell out her order. Fortunately, the pub had filled up a bit since Carole had last been at the bar. Brandie was still there. She responded warmly to the strained smile she was offered. But Ted Crisp was busy with customers, so the 'lovie' dialogue was, at least temporarily, suspended.

Back in the alcove, Vi Benyon was silent for a moment. Then she said to Jude, 'You know, this talk of Anita Garner brings it all back to me. That time, with Mum so ill. I sort of feel guilty sometimes.'

'Why? Why should you feel guilty?' asked Jude.

'I just feel, had I been concentrating, had I been more aware of what was going on at Footscrow House, I could have maybe worked out what happened to the poor girl.'

'You shouldn't blame yourself.'

'Shouldn't, I agree. But I still do. And when I think about that time, it makes me feel uncomfortable. Strange sort of feeling . . . the feeling that there's still someone around in Fethering who knows where Anita Garner is.'

'And do you still feel that, now Harry Lasalle's dead?'

'Yes. It's a kind of instinct, you know. And it's an instinct that I feel more strongly than ever. Someone in Fethering knows what happened to Anita Garner.'

Pete was used to Jude's morning routine, so when he arrived on the Thursday, one of his finishing-off days, he was surprised to find her up and dressed. She didn't mention that she had woken early, excited at the prospect of seeing him. Not a sexual excitement, an investigative one.

But she did go through the ritual of providing him with a cup of coffee (white with one sugar) before she broached what she wanted to talk about.

'Pete, remember when we found the handbag . . .?'

'Hardly going to forget about it, am I? While no one in Fethering can leave the subject alone.'

'You told me that, when you were doing that refurbishment of Footscrow House – prior to it ceasing to be a care home and becoming a boutique hotel . . .'

'Yes,' he said, puzzled. 'So, what did I say?'

'You said that you were only working on the ground floor at that time.'

'Did I? Then perhaps I was. Or perhaps that's what I remember. Jude, I've been working as a decorator for nearly forty years. You wouldn't believe the number of properties in the Fethering area I've been in and out of. And when we're talking about a place I've decorated lots of times, like Fiasco House . . . I had a call yesterday, confirming I'll be back there on Monday, painting it yet again. But, like I say, my memory for whether I painted the upstairs or the downstairs of the place, way back at the beginning of my career . . . well, my recollection could be a little bit hazy.'

He sounded completely guileless, just mildly surprised at her line of questioning. And what he said was plausible. But Jude did want to be completely sure.

'You said at the time we found the handbag, you'd never been in that room at Footscrow House before.'

'Well, I hadn't, had I?'

'I wondered if, perhaps, you'd been in part of that room.'

'"Part of . . ."?' He looked even more bewildered. 'What you on about, Jude?'

'When Footscrow House was a care home, the big upstairs rooms must've been divided into smaller units.'

'Yes, you betcha. Harry Lasalle was always trying to boost his profits. He'd fit in as many paying customers as he could. Their rooms were like rabbit hutches.' That was clearly a favourite

Fethering simile. 'Mind you, he still couldn't make a go of it as a business.' The decorator chuckled.

'So, what I'm thinking is, Pete . . . that when you painted the rooms, you didn't paint the one with the boarded-off alcove, because that was then a separate unit.' She couldn't keep a note of triumph out of her voice as she said this.

'So?' Pete looked puzzled. 'Yes, it probably was, but why's that important?'

'It's important because you said that . . .' Jude's words trickled away. She realized she couldn't go further without admitting the extent of the suspicions that she had been entertaining about Pete. And she didn't want to do that. It would seem like a betrayal. Nor could she admit how ecstatic she felt to have proved that he wasn't a liar.

'It doesn't matter,' she said, inadequately. 'What is important is that, back when Footscrow House was a care home, that room with the alcove wasn't for the residents' use.'

'Oh?' said Pete, still searching for relevance in what she was saying. He took a long swallow of coffee.

'It was used by the staff if they had to stay overnight.'

'So?' That hadn't made it relevant either.

'Well, I was thinking that Anita Garner might well have stayed in that room.'

'She was on the staff, so yes, I guess she might well have done.'

'In fact, it might well have been that room she was in immediately before she disappeared!'

'How'd'you work that out?'

Jude was forced to admit that she had no logical answer to his question. But she knew from long experience that, for her, at times instinct was more powerful than logic.

'Anyway, thank you so much, Pete.' She enveloped him in a huge, warm hug.

The toothy grin reappeared. 'What did I do to deserve that?'

She couldn't give the true answer. She couldn't tell him the magnitude of the relief she felt at having her suspicions of him allayed. So, she said, 'Just the lovely job you've done decorating my sitting room.'

'We aim to please, madam,' said Pete, in a mock-subservient voice and with a finger-tap to an invisible cloth cap.

'Now, could I get you another cup of coffee (white with one sugar)?'

'Never been known to say no, Jude,' replied the decorator.

THIRTEEN

'Is that Carole? I'm afraid I don't know your surname.'

'Seddon. Carole Seddon. Mrs Carole Seddon. Who is this?'

'My name's Fred Givens.'

'Ah.' This was promising. The fact that he was ringing her was surely promising from the point of view of their investigation.

'Yesterday my wife Lauren held a Pottery Open Day at our house.'

'Yes, I saw a flyer for it.' Carole didn't want to volunteer any more. Wait and see where he would take the conversation.

Fred Givens took it in the direction she had been afraid he would. 'Did you come to our house yesterday, Mrs Seddon?'

She couldn't tell an outright lie, but maybe it was time to ration the amount of truth. 'Yes, I did come with a friend. But there didn't seem to be anyone there, so we went away again.'

'You didn't come into the house?'

'Er . . . Well . . .'

'Mrs Seddon, I went into the studio and I saw you and your friend going out through the curtain.'

'Yes. When we saw there was no one in the studio, we turned round and—'

'Mrs Seddon, while you were in the studio, my wife and I were having a conversation in the kitchen.'

'Were you?' asked Carole innocently.

'And I'd like to know how much you and your nosy friend heard.'

It was hardly surprising that he didn't want to meet in a public place like the Crown and Anchor or Fethering Yacht Club. His own house was ruled out because Lauren was there. Pete was still finishing up in Woodside Cottage and the place smelled of paint. But, anyway, Carole would have insisted that their meeting took place at High Tor. Hypersensitive to the smallest imagined slight, she wanted to assert her role in their investigation. Fred Givens had contacted her, after all.

He got the full sitting-room treatment, with coffee things and biscuits on a tray. His manner still reflected a lifetime of urbanity, but small details suggested something had shaken him out of his customary serenity. The conversation Carole and Jude had so serendipitously overheard can't have been the first time he'd heard of his wife's infidelity, but they got the impression the shock had been relatively recent. The effects showed in the sheen of sweat on his forehead and the tremor in his hand as he picked up his coffee cup.

He and Carole had established on the phone how much information she and Jude had, but he wanted to run through the details to make sure he'd got it right.

'Obviously,' he said, 'this is not the kind of news that I want all round Fethering. So can I rely on your discretion?' There was a note of pleading in the question.

'Of course,' said Carole and Jude together. But their eyes met, exchanging the thought that, though they wouldn't deliberately spread the scandal, if it was useful in the furtherance of their investigation, that situation might change.

'You haven't discussed what you heard with anyone else?'

Both could honestly answer no to that.

'Well, please don't.'

They both again affirmed that they wouldn't.

'But it is amazing,' Carole observed, 'that your wife and Glen Porter could be having an affair without anyone knowing – in a place like Fethering.'

'It seems they were very discreet.' Fred Givens brushed the back of his hand against his sweating brow. 'I'm sorry, I get no pleasure from having to go through these sordid details. Glen, it seems, spends more of his time abroad than he does in the village, so their relationship didn't have the kind of continuity that might have drawn attention to it. They never went out anywhere, so the local snoopers wouldn't have seen them together in a restaurant or pub. She used to go to meet him in the beach hut, after dark. And only during the week, of course. Because I'd be here at the weekends, duped into imagining that I was happily married.' The bitterness in his words was painful.

'I used to enjoy my weekends. I thought I still was enjoying them, though, when I come to think about it, there were signs that Lauren was drifting away from me. We used to sail together, both members of the yacht club. She would crew for me, but recently she'd lost interest, only went to the club on sufferance. I suppose I should have recognized that as a symptom, a sign that she had developed another interest . . . like Glen Bloody Porter!'

'It was my starting to work from home more that put a damper on their cosy little relationship. Difficult for Lauren to explain to me why she suddenly had to slip out in the middle of a cosy domestic evening.' Emotion suddenly seized him. 'God, I can't imagine why I ever trusted her!'

'I understand it must be very difficult for you,' said Jude gently, 'but can I ask whether Lauren had ever had other affairs?' Her knowledge of human behaviour told her that infidelity could all too easily become a habit.

'I would have said no,' Fred replied sourly. 'I would have said no a hundred times! In fact, I never even asked myself the question. But Lauren and I have talked a lot over the last few days. And all kinds of unpleasant things have crawled out of the woodwork.'

'So, Glen wasn't the first?' asked Carole.

'No.'

Jude asked suddenly, 'Did she once have a thing going on with Harry Lasalle?'

Her neighbour's expression mixed surprise with envy. 'Extrasensory powers' were part of the mumbo-jumbo that Carole didn't believe in, but she had to admit sometimes to being astonished by Jude's intuition.

'How did you know that?' Fred Givens looked horror-struck. 'Does everyone in Fethering know?'

'No, of course not. It's just that, in the conversation we overheard, you mentioned Harry Lasalle had talked about your wife's relationship with Glen Porter. I thought his motivation might have been jealousy, you know, the ageing former lover being supplanted by the younger model.'

'Maybe.' He didn't sound convinced. 'And you're sure you've never heard people in Fethering talking about Lauren and Harry Lasalle?'

'Sure.'

'It might have been a while ago.'

'I've never heard their names mentioned in the same sentence,' said Jude.

'Nor have I,' Carole confirmed.

Fred Givens looked momentarily relieved by their responses. But his suspicion and self-laceration would not leave him alone. 'It's just the thought that everyone might have known, that all of Fethering might have been laughing at me behind their hands. They always say the husband is the last to know. Is there anyone more pathetic than the man who doesn't know his wife has been constantly cheating on him?'

'Nobody knew,' Jude soothed.

'Harry Lasalle found out about Lauren and Glen Porter. If he could find out about the affair, then so could anyone else.'

'He probably only found out because he was jealous,' suggested Jude. 'Maybe he stalked her. Followed her around to see what she was up to. Nobody else in Fethering would have bothered to do that.'

'I hope you're right,' said Fred uneasily.

Carole came in, with a harder tone. 'Of course, the situation has changed now rather, hasn't it?'

'What do you mean?'

'With Harry Lasalle's death.'

'What difference has that made?' The enquiry sounded innocent. Fred Givens hadn't caught on to the direction in which Carole's questions were leading.

She spelled it out. 'With Harry knowing about their affair, and the constant threat of him sharing the information with someone else, there could be a view that Glen Porter – or indeed your wife – might have wanted to keep him quiet.'

Still, Fred didn't cotton on. '"Keep him quiet"? How?'

'By killing him,' said Carole coolly.

'"Killing him"?' He was locked in echo mode. 'You mean – murder him?'

'There would be a logic to it,' said Carole.

'"Murder"? The general view in Fethering seems to be that he committed suicide.'

'Fethering's "general view" doesn't have a great track record for accuracy.'

'No, but . . .'

'Of course, if Harry was murdered,' Jude joined in, 'some people might reckon you would have had a motive too.'

'Really? What?' Fred appeared still to be lost in their speculations.

'Revenge on Harry? Once you discovered that he'd had an affair with your wife?'

'Oh, for heaven's sake! And how, in your scenario, would Harry have been murdered?'

'The perpetrator,' said Carole, 'would have been someone who knew about boats.'

'And the fact that I'm a member of Fethering Yacht Club puts me in the frame, does it?' Fred asked sarcastically.

'You asked how Harry could have been murdered,' Carole reprimanded him primly, 'and I am spelling out how it could have happened.'

'All right. Go on.'

'The perpetrator,' she continued, 'would have known Harry's habits, where he usually anchored *Harry's Dream* when he went out fishing. They would have gone out there in their own boat, boarded his and sabotaged the heater to start the carbon monoxide leak . . .'

'Anyone who did that would be a pretty stupid murderer,' said Fred Givens with some force.

'Why?' asked Carole, a little miffed at having her reconstruction interrupted.

'Because, if killing Harry by carbon monoxide poisoning was their plan, that would have been a very elaborate way of doing it.'

'Oh? So, how else could they have done it?'

'The simplest way,' said Fred, talking patiently as if to a child, 'would have been to organize the sabotage before the boat got on to the water.'

'Sorry?'

'Like the majority of yacht club boats, *Harry's Dream* spends most of its time on the hardstanding at the front. It sits there on its trailer with its cover on. When the owner fancies a sail, they wheel the boat down to the slipway until it floats off the trailer.

Any murderer worth his salt would have sabotaged the heater while the boat was still on land.'

Carole looked crestfallen. 'Ah yes. I suppose they would.'

But she caught a sparkle in Jude's eye and realized the implication of what Fred had just told them. If the boobytrap on *Harry's Dream* had been set up on land, it didn't have to have been done by a boat-owner. Their range of suspects had opened out considerably. It could have been anyone with a basic knowledge of the workings of Fethering Yacht Club.

Jude couldn't dispel from her mind the recollection that Lauren Givens used to crew for her husband.

She also realized – and she could see from Carole's expression that her neighbour was realizing it too – that any suspicion they might have entertained about Fred Givens being involved in Harry Lasalle's death was trickling away fast. To use his expression, no 'murderer worth his salt' would have volunteered so readily how he might have committed the crime.

Unless, of course, his openness was part of an elaborate double bluff. But neither woman thought the stolid and unimaginative Fred Givens was capable of a double bluff.

This talk of murder had briefly diverted him from his main preoccupation, the state of his marriage, but he was soon brought back to it. 'I just can't see any future for me and Lauren,' he said despairingly. 'Knowing what I now know, we can never get back to the kind of life we had before.'

'Adultery needn't always spell the end of a marriage,' said Jude reassuringly. Well, you'd know about such things, thought Carole. 'Sometimes, it can get a couple talking about aspects of their relationship they never have before. It can even strengthen the marriage.'

'Huh,' said Fred contemptuously. 'I don't see that happening with Lauren and me. Now, when I try to start a conversation with her, all she wants to talk about is bloody Glen Porter.'

'Ah,' said Jude. 'I'm sorry.'

'It's like she's been wanting to talk about him to me since the relationship began . . .'

'Do you know how long ago that was?' asked Carole.

'Four years! Four bloody years I've been walking around in

blissful ignorance, thinking I'd got a happy marriage, and all the time . . .' The pain and anger were too strong for him to finish the sentence.

'I'm sorry,' said Jude again, feeling that the word was as useless as it had been the time before.

Fred Givens took a sip of now-cold coffee, which seemed to calm him down a little. 'Anyway, now I know about the . . . affair, now there's no need for her to keep secret about it, the floodgates have really opened. Lauren's bombarding me with unwanted information about Glen Porter. As if I was interested in the details of their pillow talk . . .

'Why should I want to know what a generous person he is, how he's set up all these charitable institutions abroad and that's where most of his money goes? I don't give a damn about any of that. The only thing that concerns me about Glen Bloody Porter – and I use the word "concerns" rather than "interests" advisedly – is that he's been having an affair with my wife for the last four years. That's the piece of information about him that I wish I didn't know.'

'You'd rather you'd never found out about the affair?' asked Jude.

'I'd rather . . . I don't know! All I do know is that, now I have found out about it, the rest of my life is completely ruined.'

'I was interested,' said Carole, 'in what you said about Glen Porter's generosity. Round Fethering, if he has any reputation, it's for being selfish and tight-fisted. Everyone knows how wealthy he is, but people I know connected with local charities have tried to get donations from him and drawn a blank every time.'

'I wouldn't know about that,' said Fred. 'But Lauren doesn't want to talk about anything else. It's galling enough for a man to know he's been cheated on. Being told how much better a person his replacement is only rubs salt in the wound.'

Jude was intrigued. 'That is a new light on Glen Porter, though. Setting up charitable institutions abroad? I suppose not everyone believes that charity should begin at home.'

'I don't care what he believes,' said Fred petulantly. 'I just never want to hear his name again! Which, since he seems to be her only topic of conversation, I suppose means never seeing Lauren again.'

'Is that what you want?' asked Jude gently.

He lowered his head into his hands and raked his fingers down his forehead. 'I don't know what I want. I'm still in shock, I suppose.'

'Do you hate Lauren for what she's done?' Jude's gentle tone was maintained.

'I can't answer that. Ever since we got married, I kind of assumed that I loved her. Not something I thought about much – perhaps, in retrospect, something I should have thought about more – but if anyone had asked me – and fortunately I don't know many people who'd ask that kind of question – I'd say yes, I loved Lauren. It's hard to unpick all that in a couple of weeks.'

'I'm sure it is,' said Carole, with surprising empathy. She remembered how long it had taken her to convince herself that her marriage to David was going nowhere.

'So now,' Fred went on, 'I don't know where I am. I daren't ask Lauren if she wants to move out and shack up with lover boy. I suppose I'm afraid of the answer . . . though, equally, I don't know if that's an outcome that he would relish.' He sighed wearily. 'I'm just totally confused.'

'Lauren hasn't mentioned moving in with him?' asked Carole.

'God, she's mentioned so many things, I can hardly tell. But no, I have no recollection of her talking about moving in with him. She just goes on about how caring he is, how much more open he is than I am.'

'"Open"?'

'Yes. Apparently, among my many faults, I'm too . . . "buttoned-up" . . . that was the expression Lauren used. I've never talked to her about my feelings, never asked her about her feelings. Now she tells me. Though it seems she thought that, even before we got married. She hoped that I'd become more communicative with the passage of the years, though apparently that hasn't happened. Another black mark to me, in comparison with the new paragon, whose name I don't want to sully my lips with.

'He's sensitive. He's caring. He asks Lauren what she's feeling all the time. If I'd known that was what she'd wanted, if she'd ever told me that was what she wanted . . . well, maybe I could have offered it. I could have met her halfway, at least. But she never said anything.'

He was silent for a moment. Then he said, 'I think the fact that we found we couldn't have children is at the back of it all.'

There was a long history of pain in his words, but not something to be followed up at that moment.

'It's strange,' Carole mused, 'given the reputation that Glen Porter has round the village, that he turns out to be this caring paragon of masculine sensitivity.'

Fred grimaced. 'Well, according to Lauren, that's what he is. He shares all his secrets with her.'

'I'm sure he doesn't,' said Jude.

'What do you mean?'

'Well, at least in his wild youth, it seems that most of Glen's secrets concerned other women. He had a reputation as a proper Jack-the-Lad, working his way through the young females of Fethering. I wouldn't think those were the kind of secrets that he would want to share with a new lover.'

'According to Lauren,' said Fred, 'he did. He talked about all of the women in his past, only to make the point how much more he loved her than any of them.'

Jude could imagine that was the kind of thing a man might say to a new lover. It had been said to her on more than one occasion. And she knew it to be duplicitous nonsense, just an ingratiating masculine ploy to get more sex. But she didn't say anything.

Carole suddenly saw an opening for another part of their investigation. 'Did Glen Porter tell Lauren whether he'd ever had sex with Anita Garner?'

'He did talk about her, yes. And, according to him, they never did.'

'Have sex?'

'No.'

'Oh?'

'But he did tell Lauren that he knew what had happened to Anita Garner.'

FOURTEEN

Fortunately, Lauren Givens's phone number was on the Pottery Open Day flyer. Also fortunately, it was her mobile, not the landline. After what she had just heard from Fred, Jude wasn't sure how likely she was to find his estranged wife at home. Only a week before, of course, Jude had seen Lauren at Fethering Yacht Club. Given the events of the past seven days, Jude thought it unlikely she'd be there again the following Saturday.

When she left High Tor for Woodside Cottage, Jude hadn't told Carole what she was about to do. This wasn't being deliberately secretive, though her neighbour would of course think it was. Jude just felt she was better suited to conduct this part of the investigation. She would report back to Carole when, hopefully, she had something to report.

'Hello?' Lauren Givens's voice was taut, ready to end the call quickly if she needed to.

'Hi. It's Jude.'

'Oh yes?' Still not convinced but waiting to hear more.

'Fred came to see me and my friend Carole.'

'Did he?'

'I'm sorry to hear about your . . . problems.'

'Oh. He told you everything, did he?'

'He told us a surprising amount.'

'Bloody typical. Right through our marriage, Fred never talked to me about his feelings but he'll happily unburden himself to complete strangers.'

'The reason I'm calling you, Lauren, is because of something Fred said about you and Glen Porter.'

'Oh yes? Well, if you're thinking of adding marriage guidance counselling to your healing work, I can tell you now, you'll be wasting your time. Fred and me is over. The relationship has been moribund for a long time. Now it's officially dead.'

'I wasn't actually calling in an attempt to mend your marriage. Not part of my business.'

'Thank God you recognize that.'

'It's between the two of you. No, the reason I'm calling is about something Fred said Glen Porter told you.'

'Oh?' The suspicion in Lauren's voice had eased a little over the past few exchanges but now it was back at reinforced strength. 'And what was that?'

'Apparently, he told you he knew what had happened to Anita Garner.'

Instantly, the line went dead. Slowly, Jude replaced the receiver on its cradle.

Hoping her prediction of what would happen next was correct, she sat down and waited.

She thought she was right. Within ten minutes, her phone rang. But the caller wasn't the one she was expecting. It was Carole.

'Jude, I thought I'd let you know that I've enlisted help.'

'"Help"? Sorry, what do you mean?'

'Now we've got a definite lead on Anita Garner's disappearance . . .'

'I'm not sure that we have quite got that.'

Carole steamrollered on, 'I thought we needed help from someone who knows more about the case than anyone else.'

'You don't mean you've been in touch with the police?' Jude was appalled. If there were any rules in the business of being an amateur detective, the predominant one was never to consult the police. The 'proper authorities' had no place in the world of untutored sleuthdom.

'No, of course I haven't,' said Carole curtly. 'I have enlisted the help of my journalist friend, Malk Penberthy.'

'Oh.'

Jude must have sounded underwhelmed because Carole went straight into reassurance mode. 'He covered the case at the time she actually disappeared. He talked to all the relevant people. He really does know more about it than anyone else.'

'Possibly. So, what have you actually told him?'

'I've told him that we know the identity of the person who holds the key to the case,' said Carole enthusiastically.

'Have you actually said it's Glen Porter?'

'No. I said I'd wait until I talked to you before I gave him the name.'

'Thank God for that,' was Jude's immediate thought. What she said, though, was, 'Can you hold fire till after the weekend?'

'Why?' Carole sounded miffed and disappointed.

'Just, please do. There are a couple of things I need to sort out.'

'"Things" that will take you the whole weekend? I thought we were doing this investigation together.' Carole was moving into full martyr mode.

'Please, Carole. If I can get them sorted sooner, I'll let you know immediately.'

'Very well.' The words were said in Carole's unique way of saying that things were far from 'very well'.

After their call ended, Jude didn't feel comfortable. It was a kind of role reversal. Usually, Carole was the one who was hypersensitive about potential slights, about the idea that she was being excluded from any part of their investigation. But now Jude was getting something of that feeling.

She knew her neighbour well enough to understand what was going on. Carole had cultivated Malk Penberthy as her own private source, someone separate from Jude. She hadn't suggested even introducing the two of them.

Jude still felt uneasy about their recently acquired information being shared with a third party.

But then a thought came to her of how the situation could be used to her advantage.

Shortly after, came the call she had been expecting. Her conjecture had been proved right. Her mention of Anita Garner had prompted Lauren Givens to contact her lover immediately.

'Hello, Jude. This is Glen Porter.'

'Hello.'

'I gather you've been stirring things up again.'

'Ooh, I don't think I'd go as far as that.'

'I would. More meddlesome talk about Anita Garner.'

'Did Lauren say why I'd raised the name?'

'Yes. She was stupid. Something I mentioned to her in confidence – and then she goes and tells her bloody husband!'

'So, you're not denying you said it?'

'No, I'm not. But I am telling you to put a stop to all this destructive gossip.'

'I'm not sure that I can.'

'What do you mean?'

'There's already a journalist sniffing round the case.'

'Bloody hell!'

'A very pertinacious journalist. One who won't rest until he finds out the truth.' This was perhaps bigging up Malk Penberthy excessively, but Jude knew what she was doing. She wasn't going to spoil her little plan by mentioning the journalist's age or the fact that he had been long retired.

It worked. 'Can you come to the beach hut?' asked Glen Porter.

There had been a sprinkling of snow that morning. It hadn't settled on the sand, just dusted the rooftops of the village. It certainly accentuated the Chekhovian look of the beach hut. The cold stung Jude's cheeks as she crossed Fethering Beach.

She had half-expected Lauren to be there, but Glen was on his own.

No offers of coffee this time. Straight to business.

'This journalist you talked about . . . what's his name?'

'I'm afraid I can't tell you that.'

'Why not?'

'He asked me not to.' Jude was not above telling the odd white lie in the cause of justice.

'Lauren swore blind to me that Fred was the only person she'd told that I'd said I knew what happened to Anita Garner.'

'Yes.'

'Did he tell you anything more than that?'

'No.'

'Are you sure?'

'Absolutely sure. But it was sufficient to spark my interest.'

'Yes,' said Glen wryly. 'I'm getting the impression it doesn't take much to do that.'

'Maybe not.'

'So, Jude, what's the current state of play? Should I be preparing myself for a call from said journalist?'

Time for a bit of tactical white lying. 'That may not happen for a while. May not happen at all.'

'Sorry, what do you mean? You said he was "sniffing around" Anita's disappearance.'

'Yes. Let me explain. I haven't met him. He's known to my neighbour Carole. Do you know who I mean?'

'Oh yes. Fethering's other menopausal meddler. I know about her.'

Jude didn't react to the insult. Time for another white lie. 'Because Carole's journalist friend knows we're interested in the case, he's offered to help us. It was through her that I got the message he didn't want his name bandied about. It's certainly a name you'd recognize,' she lied blithely. 'He's got quite a reputation for investigative journalism.'

'Has he? And your friend Carole asked him to help solve Anita Garner's disappearance?'

'She hasn't yet said definitely whether she wants him to or not.' Another lie easily slipped in. 'That's why I said his intervention may not happen.'

'Ah.' A light of hope came into Glen Porter's eyes. 'So, he could still be headed off, could he?'

'Might be possible,' said Jude, deliberately capricious.

'I would be very grateful if you could head him off,' said Glen firmly.

'How grateful?'

'What do you mean? For God's sake! Are you asking me for money?'

'No.' Jude was shocked that he might think that. But then she reflected that someone chiefly known locally for being rich must get many such requests. It would be reasonable to assume that money was what everyone was after.

'No,' she repeated. 'I'm asking for information. You're not about to deny that you know what happened to Anita, are you?'

'No. But I have reasons for keeping that information secret.'

'Really? I wonder what they could be . . .?'

'I don't think it's really your business, Jude.'

'Perhaps not. But I can't stop myself from being intrigued by it.'

'Evidently not,' Glen said drily. 'I imagine there are few things you can stop yourself being intrigued by.'

'You're probably right. But listen, your reasons for keeping the information you have about Anita Garner secret . . .'

'Yes?'

'The way I see it, either you'd want secrecy to avoid incriminating yourself . . .'

'Oh, last time it was Harry Lasalle I was supposed to have bumped off. You're accusing me of murdering the girl now, are you?'

'No, I'm not.'

'I'm relieved to hear that. There were so many nasty allegations going round just after her disappearance, I don't want all that starting up again.'

'All right, Glen, but just bear with me a moment. If you had murdered her and knew where the body was hidden, then fine, that'd be a reason for keeping the facts secret.'

'I would go along with that.' In spite of the potential seriousness of the situation, he was enjoying this intellectual sparring. 'And if – just to offer a more charitable interpretation of my behaviour – I didn't murder her . . . what then?'

'Then, the reason for your silence could be that you know who did murder her and are keeping quiet to avoid shopping them.'

'I understand the logic of that, yes.'

'There are other possibilities,' said Jude.

'Mm. Infinite numbers, I would imagine.'

Jude decided she needed more facts. 'What has prompted all this speculation over the years is that nobody knows what was the precise nature of your relationship with Anita Garner at the time.'

'No, they don't . . . however much they invent scenarios of romance and loathing. Nobody knows anything. And, for me, that seems a very satisfactory state of affairs. And one whose continuation I see no reason to stop.'

'Maybe not. You know Vi Benyon?'

'Do I?'

'Mother of Kent, who you were at school with.'

'Oh yes. Then I know who you mean.'

'According to Vi, Kent said that you "got inside Anita's knickers".'

'Good old Kent. I wonder where he got his information from.'

Glen didn't seem inclined to continue, so Jude pressed on, 'Apparently, you had quite a reputation as a Jack-the-Lad back then, working your way through the adoring young women of Fethering.'

He gave a wry smile, not of triumphalism, more of doubt. 'That reputation was, I suppose, justified at the time. Like most young men, I enjoyed sex and wasn't too bothered about the emotional side of things.'

'Are you implying you've changed?'

'Yes. Sex without emotional engagement has lost its lustre for me.'

'So, your relationship with Lauren—?'

'We are not here to talk about my relationship with Lauren. We are her to talk about my relationship – if any – with Anita Garner.'

'Very well. So, what was it?' asked Jude bluntly.

'I'm not particularly proud of my behaviour in my late teens and early twenties. My approach to women was very much of the "notches on the bedpost" variety. I have changed considerably since then.'

Jude, ever the investigator of human behaviour, couldn't restrain herself from asking, 'What caused the change?'

Glen Porter grinned. 'My suddenly becoming wealthy. You hear frequently that "money is the root of all evil".'

'To be accurate, "the love of money is the root of all kinds of evil",' Jude pointed out.

'I stand corrected. Anyway, in my case, the reverse proved to be true. My acquisition of money was the root of all good in me. For the first time, I had the freedom to ask myself what I really wanted from life. I no longer had to scrape a living, working behind bars, stacking shelves, portering in hospitals. I could leave Fethering. I could do things.'

'So, what "things" did you do?'

'First thing was to go to university. It had never been an option before. My parents hardly knew what a university was, and the local comprehensive wasn't exactly grooming its students for academia. So, first I did evening classes to get the requisite A levels, then spent three mind-expanding years doing English and Philosophy at the University of Liverpool.

'And, perhaps being that much older than most of the under-graduate intake, I didn't immediately embark on an orgy of wild promiscuity. I had already been through that phase of my life. Instead, I learned to take relationships more seriously, to realize – perhaps for the first time – that the other person involved was a sentient being too.'

'Quite a breakthrough,' said Jude drily.

'Yes, it was. I also spent a lot of time thinking about how I should spend my unexpected fortune.'

'Fethering thinks you spend it on living the high life abroad. Mention your name and expressions like "splash the cash" and "playboy" will infallibly occur in the next sentence.'

'If you think I give a shit what Fethering thinks, Jude, then you have seriously misjudged my character.'

'I haven't had much of a chance to make a judgement about your character.'

'No. Nor I yours. You were, however, I should point out, quite recently willing to believe me capable of murdering Harry Lasalle.'

'Yes,' said Jude with mock-winsomeness. 'But I didn't know you so well then.'

That earned a grin. Though she still didn't fancy him physic-ally, Jude found herself attracted at an intellectual level.

'Anyway,' she went on, 'I know more about how education transformed your character' – another grin from him – 'but I still don't know the nature of your relationship with Anita Garner.'

'Very well. I'll tell you. It's a disappointing answer . . . for lovers of the prurient. Nothing happened. I never made love to her.'

'And was that . . . for lovers of the accurate . . . not for want of trying?'

'You're right, I'm afraid. I did regard her as a challenge, back in what you would probably call my "Jack-the-Lad" phase. I took her out a couple of times. But I didn't get anywhere.'

'Could you be more specific?'

'God, you ask a lot, Jude. Are you asking for details of my every thwarted fumble?'

'That's exactly what I'm asking for.'

'Very well then. Since you have such a persuasive manner . . . I will tell you that I came on to her very heavily. I had certain techniques which had proved effective with other girls. None of us had our own places back then. We mostly still lived with our parents, so opportunities for . . . what? Carnal interaction? Such opportunities were rare. I was a bit ahead of the pack. I had my own van. That was the scene of most of my . . . what shall I call them?'

'Conquests?' Jude suggested.

'I suppose so. Sounds a bit shabby in these post-MeToo days.'

'Were probably pretty shabby at the time.'

'Yes. Thank you, Jude. I'm sure I deserved that.'

'Anyway, you and Anita . . .?'

'Basically, I came up against the brick wall of her religion. Catholicism has a lot to answer for when it comes to sex. If you ban contraception, you're bound to cause poverty and domestic violence. If you insist on a celibate priesthood, you cannot fail to engender paedophilia. But you don't want to get me started on all that.'

'No, I certainly don't. Let's just talk about you and Anita.'

'OK. Well, as I said, I came on to her. I tried to seduce her. She wouldn't let me. Sex before marriage was against her religion. I think she did genuinely believe that. I think also, though, she was terrified of her father. He was the one who – literally – put the fear of God into her. She said if he found out she'd had sex before marriage – even worse, if she were to get pregnant before she got married – he would turn her out of the house and cut off all communication with her.'

This conformed with everything else Jude had heard about the late Mr Garner. 'Tell me, Glen,' she asked, 'did Anita ever have a boyfriend?'

'Not that I heard of. Certainly not one she went to bed with, I'm pretty sure of that.'

'Hm. The name "Pablo" doesn't mean anything to you?'

'No. In what context?'

'He was someone Anita worked with at a pub called the Cat

and Fiddle. We heard from the former landlady of the place that they were very close.'

Glen Porter shook his head. 'Never heard anything about that.' Then he seemed to feel they'd done enough intellectual skirmishing. 'Can we get back to this journalist of yours, Jude?'

'By all means.'

'For reasons of my own . . . yes, I've said that before – but you've got to believe me, they are solid, humanitarian reasons – I don't want the investigation of Anita Garner's disappearance restarted. And I certainly don't want your hotshot journalist sniffing round the case. That could only cause a lot of distress.'

'Distress to whom?'

'The individuals concerned,' he replied unhelpfully. 'But you seem to have come here to bargain, Jude. We've established you don't want money. So, what is your price for not unleashing your high-powered investigative journalist?'

'According to Lauren, passed on to us by her husband, you know what happened to Anita Garner.' There was a silence. 'Are you denying that?'

'No, I'm not.'

'You asked what my price is. My price is you telling me what you know, you telling me what happened to Anita Garner.'

'Then you'll not give your journalist my name?'

'Definitely won't, no.'

'And see that my name is kept out of further investigations by you and your nosy neighbour?'

'You have my word on it.'

Glen Porter was silent for a moment, assessing his options. Then he said, 'All right.'

And he told Jude what had happened to Anita Garner.

Jude felt pretty good on the icy walk back to Woodside Cottage. Her little plan had worked.

And she thought Malk Penberthy, formerly of the *Fethering Observer*, might have been flattered by being presented as someone with the combined investigative skills of Carl Bernstein and Bob Woodward from *All the President's Men* – and better than either of them.

As for the lies she had told to achieve her desired result, she felt no guilt about them. Truth was, as ever, a justifiable casualty in pursuit of the greater good.

Her only small disquiet arose from the condition Glen Porter had insisted on before he gave her the information. That she mustn't share it with anyone. Not even Carole. Though in fact that suited her own intentions well, she knew it would inevitably lead to conflict some way down the line.

FIFTEEN

Carole Seddon slept fitfully that Saturday night. She wasn't quite sure what she felt. While cheered by her excellent idea of getting Malk Penberthy on board, she was less cheered by Jude's demand for a delay in the investigation. Always potentially paranoid, Carole got the feeling that something was being kept from her. She decided that, when she and Malk Penberthy did finally get on to Glen Porter's case, she might withhold some of their findings from Jude. Two could play at the secrecy game.

On the Sunday morning, after she'd taken Gulliver for his constitutional on an Antarctic Fethering Beach, as soon as they returned to High Tor, she rang through to Woodside Cottage. There was no reply.

Knowing – and disapproving – of Jude's lax morning regime (particularly lax at weekends), she went round and knocked on the front door. No response. Where had Jude gone without telling her?

In a fit of pique, Carole rang Malk Penberthy. She wasn't about to break the undertaking she'd given to Jude and give him Glen Porter's name, but she reckoned there were other advances the two of them might make on the investigation.

By half past eleven, Starbucks was like the interior of a cocoon, toasty warm, with the outside world shut off by condensation on the windows.

Though forbidden from telling Malk about Fred Givens's final revelation, Carole saw no reason why she shouldn't share other details they had learned from the distraught husband. The old journalist was interested to hear about Lauren Givens's affair with Glen Porter, but clearly couldn't see what relevance it had to their investigation of Anita Garner's disappearance. Carole felt very frustrated by not being able to explain the full situation to him, but she kept her word to Jude.

There were other areas she could go into, though. 'One interesting thought that Fred Givens did plant in our minds, though, was how the sabotage on *Harry's Dream* could have been effected.'

'Oh?'

'If we're following the scenario that Harry Lasalle was murdered . . .'

'Last time we discussed his death, I thought we were favouring the scenario of suicide.'

'Yes, but murder is another possibility.'

'I suppose so.' He thought it through. 'Someone other than its owner sabotaged the heater on *Harry's Dream*?'

'Exactly. And Jude and I were trying to think who might have sailed out to where Harry was anchored and—'

'Why would they bother doing that? Be much simpler to sabotage the boat on land, while it was at Fethering Yacht Club.'

Carole felt suitably chastened. Both Fred Givens and now Malk Penberthy had reached the same obvious conclusion, the one that she and Jude hadn't.

Malk went on, 'But, following your scenario, who would want Harry Lasalle dead?'

'Well, if the secret of his affair with Anita Garner was about to be revealed . . .'

'Which was thought of as a motive for him to top himself . . .'

'Yes, but it might as easily have been a motive for someone to kill him.'

'Why?'

'Revenge, maybe?' She knew as she said the words how feeble they sounded.

'Yes. I find a more plausible possibility – if we're talking murder – is that someone set up the death deliberately to look like suicide . . .'

'With a view to . . .?'

'Silencing Harry? Stopping the truth coming out? Stopping him from incriminating someone else?'

'The murderer?'

'Quite possibly, Carole, yes.' After his initial scepticism, Malk was now becoming enthused by the murder theory. 'So, who would be our suspects? To have access to the hardstanding where

Harry's Dream was, they'd have to be members of Fethering Yacht Club.'

'Why's that?'

'Security's tight there. Those boats are quite valuable. Not so much likelihood of their being stolen, but vandalism was always a worry at the yacht club. Way back in the day, when I was reporting for the *Fethering Observer*, I covered a good few break-ins there – some just to nick booze from the bar. Then I also reported on the new security system the yacht club brought in. CCTV and what-have-you. They were keen there should be lots of coverage for that in the *Observer*, a warning to any potential vandals about the risks they'd be taking. Later, they upgraded to a key-card system. Only someone with a card could get in.

'So, what we have to ask ourselves is . . . which members of Fethering Yacht Club might have had a motive to kill Harry Lasalle?'

'Apparently, somehow Harry knew about the affair between Glen Porter and Lauren Givens. Either of them might have wanted to silence him,' suggested Carole, hoping Malk wasn't about to go down the route of suspecting Glen.

To her relief, he replied, 'She has more at stake than he does. Glen's unmarried. Lauren has a marriage that is capable of being destroyed . . . which, from your account, is what has happened to it.'

'And we know both Givenses are members of the yacht club.'

'Yes, Fred and Lauren made a big fuss about some new boat they'd bought when they first came down here. So, who're our other suspects?'

'Apparently, Pete the decorator is a member of the yacht club.'

'And what motive might he have for topping Harry Lasalle?'

'No idea. Though it seems there's bad blood between him and the old boy's widow.'

'What about her as a suspect? The stony-faced Veronica? Most murders seem to emerge from the cradle of family relationships.'

'They certainly do, Malk. Which of course could bring Roland Lasalle into the equation. I don't know whether he would still be a member of the yacht club. He used to be, in his teens, I think. Crewed for his father. But he's hardly set foot in Fethering since then. Only come back now he's masterminding the newest version of Fiasco House. He's worth bearing in mind, though.'

'Possibly, Carole. Though, if one were considering the immediate family, I wouldn't look much further than Veronica.'

'Oh?'

'From all accounts, Harry led her a merry dance in their early years together. Constant infidelities. Jury's still out on whether he actually had an affair with Anita Garner, but there were plenty of others there's no doubt about. I think Veronica's firmly in the frame. "Hell hath no fury . . ." and all that. What's more, she's definitely a member of the yacht club. Used to crew for her husband. And, of course, she provided his alibi for the time of Anita's disappearance. Both of them in *Harry's Dream*, sailing to France.'

'But why, suddenly, should she turn on him? After, what, forty years of marriage? Possibly more. Why now?'

'Perhaps,' Malk Penberthy suggested, 'the prospect of all the Anita Garner rumours being raked over again was more than she could face. Perhaps,' he continued, entranced by the new thought, 'she knew that her husband had killed Anita and she couldn't face the prospect of the truth coming out . . .?'

'I suppose it's possible.' But Carole didn't sound convinced.

'It's more than possible,' said a conspiratorial Malk Penberthy. 'No question about it, for me the prime suspect is Veronica Lasalle.'

A new thought came to Carole Seddon. A rare beam expanded her thin lips.

'Malk,' she said, 'would you allow me to buy you lunch at the Crown and Anchor?'

Sunday lunchtime was traditionally one of the pub's busiest times, but that did not apply in a cold February. The villagers of Fethering were still in the post-Christmas social slump, when their own firesides and home-cooked meals held more appeal than going out.

Granted, it was only just after opening time when Carole and Malk arrived. The individual she was hoping to meet wasn't yet there. In fact, the only person in the bar was Ted Crisp, lugubriously polishing glasses.

'What can I get you to drink, Malk?' Carole asked.

'I apologize for letting down the image of the hard-drinking journalist for you, but I'll just have a half of ginger beer shandy.'

'Fine. Take a seat. I'll get some menus.'

She crossed to the bar. Ted looked up from his polishing. She was shocked to observe that his hair and beard were neatly trimmed. Another manifestation of the Brandie Effect, she surmised. She gave Malk's order.

'And it'll be a large New Zealand Sauvignon Blanc for you.'

'Oh, I think just a small one.'

'Large,' said the landlord, proceeding to pour it.

She didn't argue but asked for two menus.

Though unwilling to mention the name, she couldn't help herself from asking, 'And how's your little friend?'

The look Ted flashed at her made her wish she hadn't asked. He seemed to be raising the possibility that she might be jealous of Brandie. Carole and the landlord's brief affair had been out of character for both of them and was almost never mentioned. Her question had clumsily resurrected it.

But Ted did not follow up on his look. He just answered evenly, 'Brandie's away for the weekend. In Wales, doing a course about Homeopathy.'

'Oh. Right.' Putting the menus under her arm, Carole picked up the drinks. 'I'll come back when we've decided what we're going to eat.'

'Fine.'

It was a new menu. Ed Pollack, the Crown and Anchor's brilliant chef, changed it every couple of weeks, even during the winter off-season. Carole was unamused to see there was now a 'Vegan Option' of 'Shepherdless Pie'. Brandie really had got her claws deep into Ted Crisp.

While they were deciding what to order, the pub door clattered open to admit Barney Poulton.

'Hello, Barney,' said Carole fulsomely.

He looked momentarily taken aback. She had never greeted him directly before and, from what he had observed of her, 'fulsome' was not her natural manner.

Quickly recovering, he returned her greeting. She made a fuss of introducing Malk Penberthy, still in fulsome mode. Then she astonished the new arrival even more by saying, 'Won't you join us? Can I get you a drink?'

The second question surprised him more than the first. During the winter, Barney Poulton generally had to buy his own drinks. In the summer months, day-trippers and tourists, fooled by his 'local character' pose, might offer him a pint in the hope of more authentic storytelling. But most Fethering villagers recognized him for the bore he was and curbed their generosity. Though he projected himself as not only 'the eyes and ears of Fethering', but also 'the life and soul of the Crown and Anchor', Barney Poulton in fact had few genuine friends in the village.

'Well, thank you very much, Carole,' he said. 'Just ask Ted for "Barney's usual".'

The landlord had started pulling the predictable pint before she reached the bar. She gave the food order. Fish and chips for her, and for Malk just 'Soup of the Day (Tomato and Coriander) with Crusty Bread'. 'I don't have a big appetite these days,' he'd said, once again prompting the question about how old he actually was.

Carole was working on the assumption that once their food arrived, Barney Poulton would take up his usual post at the bar, so she wanted to plant ideas in his head as soon as possible.

It wasn't difficult to get him on to the subject of Harry Lasalle's death. Once they were there, she asked if he'd heard any new theories about what had caused it. As ever, he had a stock of dodgy insider knowledge to impart.

'The Fethering consensus seems to be moving towards suicide, but of course the interesting question that raises is what caused him to take his own life. And the general view seems to be that he couldn't face the shame of having his affair with Anita Garner exposed.'

'Oh?' asked Malk Penberthy. 'I followed the case at the time. As Carole just said, I was a journalist on the *Fethering Observer*. I heard lots of rumours about Anita Garner and Harry Lasalle but could never get any of them substantiated. You have proof, do you, that they definitely did have an affair?'

'Not proof as such,' Barney replied evasively, 'but I'm pretty sure it happened.'

Carole didn't ask on what assumption this was based. He was

moving very satisfactorily in the direction she wanted him to go and she had no wish to divert him.

'So, Barney,' she asked, 'do you think it was just the revelation of the affair that Harry was worried about?'

'No, obviously there was more to it than that.'

'What more?'

Barney Poulton looked cautiously around the nearly empty pub before replying. And then it was in a whisper. 'Obviously, the fact that he had done away with Anita Garner.'

'Oh, you have proof he did *that*, do you?' asked Malk.

'Again, not actual proof, but I've no doubt that's what happened.'

'Right.' The old journalist sounded less than convinced. He didn't point out that, having spent a lot of professional time reporting on the disappearance when it happened, he might know more about the subject than someone who'd only lived in Fethering for the past four years.

'Hm,' said Carole. 'You're probably right, Barney.' Something that she didn't for a minute believe. 'And that might tie in with another rumour I heard recently.'

'Oh?' He was all ears. 'What was that?'

'Well . . . if Harry Lasalle did murder Anita Garner . . .'

'Which I'm damned sure he did. Her body'll be out on the South Downs somewhere. In a shallow grave. If the police only took their job seriously, they'd realize . . .'

A look from Carole dried up his words, as she went on, 'If he did, then he might not be the only one afraid of the truth getting out.'

'Sorry?'

'Members of his family,' she explained, 'might also want to keep it quiet. They wouldn't want all that adverse publicity. And the police tend to lose interest in cases where their chief suspect is dead.'

'Ah.' Enlightenment dawned on Barney Poulton. 'You mean his wife might have got him out of the way?'

'I was thinking more of the son,' Carole lied. 'Roland Lasalle has a reputation to maintain, as an internationally known architect. He wouldn't want his image sullied by sordid revelations about his father.'

She watched the idea take root in Barney Poulton's mind. 'No, you're right, he wouldn't,' he said slowly.

Just at that moment, their food arrived, delivered by Zosia, the bar manager. During the chat with her, Barney saw some acquaintances arrive and, with thanks to Carole for the drink, went across to take his customary pontificating chair by the bar.

While she addressed her fish and chips, and Malk Penberthy addressed his 'Soup of the Day (Tomato and Coriander) with Crusty Bread', Carole kept an eye on Barney Poulton, as ever chatting away to anyone who would listen (and a good few who'd rather not). She felt confident that her little plan would work.

It was some years since Jude had been on a long train journey. As she watched the flat landscape slide past the window, she felt a familiar restlessness. She didn't get out of Fethering enough. Maybe it was time for a new challenge in her life. Time to move on yet again.

And her restlessness was compounded by the thought of the challenge that lay ahead of her that day.

Carole's little plan was based on her knowledge of the way Fethering worked. Particularly on the way the village grapevine worked. It was still a constant source of wonder to her, the speed with which a rumour could travel round the entire population.

And she reckoned, when it came to the dissemination of rumours, Barney Poulton definitely qualified as the Fethering champion.

Back at High Tor from the Crown and Anchor, she had misgivings, though. Her confidence, always fragile, began to wobble. She wondered whether her little plan had been so clever, after all. It had been purely speculative, there was no guarantee that it would work.

But, just before three thirty, it happened. There was a furious thumping on the front door.

Carole opened it. On her doorstep, as anticipated, stood a very angry Veronica Lasalle.

SIXTEEN

The address in Liverpool was up near the Anglican cathedral. After her early start from Fethering Station, Jude arrived at around two in the afternoon. She thought about stopping for something to eat but rejected the idea. What she had to do was her first priority. There'd be time for food afterwards.

Glen Porter had given her a phone number as well as the address, but Jude felt disinclined to use it. From what he had told her, she got the impression that her quarry was of a nervous disposition, likely to take fright and hide away if she had warning of a stranger's arrival.

The area looked almost middle class, well-maintained houses with neat, small front gardens. Little was growing there in February, but the care with which the plants were tended suggested that spring would bring a profusion of flowers. Nothing looked opulent, everything looked respectable.

But the shabbier streets Jude walked through as she climbed St James's Mount, the empty bottles and other detritus she saw on the pavements and in the gutters, suggested a darker side to the area. She got the feeling it might be less welcoming after dark.

The house whose address she had been given was divided into two flats, one on each floor. '74A' was at ground level. With trepidation, Jude pressed the plastic bell push.

It wasn't an encounter for which she could have done much useful preparation. As so often in her life, she would have to react instinctively to whatever she was presented with.

The door was opened by a woman about her own age. She was dressed in dark blue, shirt, skirt, tights. A grey cardigan against the cold. Shoes so sensible they could have started a Neighbourhood Watch.

Her hair, that fine white which had once been blonde, was swept back into a kind of Alice band. The impression she gave was of being in a kind of uniform, an acolyte of some religious order perhaps.

'Hello?' she said. Her voice had the slightest Scouse nasal twang.

'Mary White?'

'Yes. And you must be Jude.'

It was a huge relief. Glen Porter had been in touch, warning the woman of her prospective visitor.

'Come in. I'm sure you could use a cuppa.'

The sitting room was at the front, bare, austere. And chilly. If there was any central heating on, it was turned down low. The furniture was functional, a rather bony three-piece suite. A few dark-bound books on a shelf, no fiction. Nothing on the walls except an anaemic print of St Francis of Assisi.

Mary White brought the tea things through on a tray from the kitchen. Jude was relieved to see there was a plate of digestive biscuits.

Her hostess's unease showed in the trembling of her hands as she poured the tea into two mugs. They still shook as Mary raised hers to her lips.

'I'm only seeing you,' she said, 'because Glen asked me to. I wouldn't do it otherwise. He said there was a reason you needed to talk to me . . .'

A relieved 'Ah' from Jude.

'. . . but he didn't tell me what it was.'

'Right.' Jude wasn't sure where to start. The handbag? The gossip? The accusations? She decided to come in at a very basic level. 'As he probably told you, I live in Fethering . . .'

'Yes.'

'And there's been a suspicious death down there recently.'

'Oh?'

'A man called Harry Lasalle.'

Mary White gave no reaction to the name. Either she had never heard it or was skilled in controlling her emotions. Another possibility was that Glen Porter had mentioned the builder's death and she had been prepared for the news.

Jude pressed, 'Does the name mean anything to you?'

The woman gave a brief shake of her head.

'Let me try another tack. A couple of weeks ago, in a building in Fethering called Footscrow House, I found a handbag.'

'So?'

'It contained a passport belonging to a woman called Anita Garner.'

'What's all this got to do with me?'

Jude had had enough of this fencing. 'What it has to do with you, Mary White, is that you are not Mary White.'

'I don't know what you mean.'

'You do. So, it's time to stop pretending. Glen told me your true identity.'

'No!'

'Yes. You are Anita Garner.'

The woman burst into tears.

'I've been here in Liverpool,' she said after Jude had soothed her back to coherence, 'ever since I left Fethering.'

'Thirty years ago?'

'Round that, yes.'

'Why Liverpool?'

'It was a long way from Fethering.'

'Were you aware of all the press interest in your disappearance?'

'Not really. I knew there must be some, but I was a long way away. I tried to avoid reading the papers and watching the television news. I was not in a very good place back then.'

'Presumably you knew the state your parents must have been in?'

'I kind of knew but shut my mind to it. I wasn't very coherent.'

'But what did you live on? Where did you live, come to that?'

'I had a bit of cash with me, though most of that went on the train fare. The first few nights up here, I slept rough. Then I got bar work. I was used to that. It was a job I could do without thinking. Which was just as well, because at the time I didn't want to think.'

Sudden fear came into the woman's face. 'Glen said I should see you. But why are you here? You're not about to tell the police who I really am?'

'No, of course I'm not. You haven't committed any crime. At least, as far as I know you haven't. There's no law against changing your name and starting a new life.'

'No. No, there isn't.' But she didn't sound certain about it.

'I can assure you, I have no desire to upset you. If you want to continue being here as Mary White, that's your business and not mine. All I'm interested in is establishing the circumstances of Harry Lasalle's death. It would appear to have been suicide. That's certainly the verdict of his wife Veronica. But there are rumours going around Fethering of murder.'

'Always rumours going round Fethering,' said the woman wryly. 'One of the reasons why I left.'

Jude was desperate to know what the other reasons were, but she didn't want to rush things. Mary White/Anita Garner was clearly highly strung and capable of clamming up at any moment.

'Yes. Look, Mary' – better to stick with her chosen identity – 'I do want to ask you some questions, but if there's anything that is too intrusive, or that you don't want to answer for any reason . . . well, that's fine with me. I'm not here to invade your privacy.'

'No.' The tone implied that Jude already had invaded her privacy. 'I'm only seeing you because Glen said I should. He suggested that if I answered your questions, that would avoid a much more public enquiry into my life.'

Jude felt pleased – and just a little bit guilty – that her mendacious approach to Glen Porter had worked so well.

She was about to start on the few, inadequate questions she had been planning on her way from Lime Street Station when Mary came in with one of her own. 'Where was my handbag found?'

'As I said, it was in Footscrow House.'

'*Where* in Footscrow House?'

'It was hidden in a boarded-up alcove, in a room which, apparently, back when the place had been a care home, had been used as a staff bedroom.'

Mary White let out a little involuntary gasp. The colour left her face.

'One thing intrigued me,' Jude went on. 'Well, many things intrigued me about your handbag, but the dominant one is the presence of your passport in it.'

'Why particularly?'

'Because, from all accounts, you'd never been abroad and had no intention of going abroad.'

'Perhaps not, but a passport's a useful thing to have . . . you know, as a proof of identity or . . .' The argument sounded pretty feeble.

'So, you weren't secretly planning to go abroad at that time?'

'No. Why would I want to do that?'

'Possibly to meet up with Pablo?'

Her face turned what could only be described as a whiter shade of pale.

'How on earth do you know about Pablo?'

'I killed Harry,' said Veronica Lasalle.

She sat upright on a kitchen chair in High Tor. The Aga spread warmth, Gulliver snored snugly in front of it, but the atmosphere was far from relaxed.

'Why are you telling me?' asked Carole. She wanted to know if it was the payoff to her plan, apart from anything else.

The response from Veronica confirmed it, very gratifyingly. 'Because you've been spreading rumours in the Crown and Anchor, rumours about Roland.'

Not for the first time, Carole was astonished by the speed of the Fethering grapevine. She had chosen well in using Barney Poulton as a conduit for the false information.

'I thought,' Veronica went on, 'I could get away with it. I thought everyone would accept the conclusion that Harry had taken his own life. But the gossip about it being murder started to spread. I hoped it'd die down. But it didn't. And, once people – well, not "people" – *you*' – she larded the pronoun with contempt – 'once you started spreading accusations about Roly, I knew I had to confess the truth.'

Though Veronica Lasalle was furiously angry, she showed no other emotions which might be expected from a woman who had recently killed her husband. No regret, no contrition, no shock and certainly no guilt.

'So, why did you do it, Veronica?' asked Carole.

'To save Harry the unhappiness which the inevitable investigation would have caused him.'

'What investigation?'

'All that business about Anita Garner suddenly getting revived. It would have destroyed him.'

Carole couldn't help saying, 'So you took it upon yourself to destroy him first?'

'If you want to put it that way, yes. Though, personally, I see it as an act of mercy.'

'Oh?'

'Listen, I'm not pretending that Harry and I had a great marriage. Yes, early on it was good. We did everything together, spent all our spare time sailing, and he never looked at another woman. But, after Roly was born . . . well, I was busy with him and perhaps hadn't got so much time to devote to Harry and . . . anyway, that was when he started to stray. The business was doing well, he was doing jobs further away from Fethering, sometimes he had to stay overnight . . . It's a familiar pattern, has happened in many marriages, I'm sure. But Harry got into the habit of infidelity.

'And I'm not saying there weren't faults on both sides. I was preoccupied with Roland, and I think that made Harry feel excluded. And I hadn't got the time to spend crewing for him on *Harry's Dream* at weekends and . . . anyway, we drifted apart. And he drifted towards other women.'

'And was one of those "other women" Anita Garner?'

Veronica Lasalle nodded grimly. 'Yes. Yes, she was. And that hurt me more than all the others. I didn't know any of the others. I knew *about* them but I didn't *know* them personally. He met them when he was away from Fethering. He was a bastard in many ways, but at least Harry didn't like to foul his own footpath, which was a kind of relief to me.

'But with Anita Garner . . . well, he was bringing his dirty linen home and displaying it for everyone in Fethering to see. Harry and I were running Footscrow House as a care home together. And then suddenly he's taking up with a member of the staff and, though they managed to keep it quiet at first, very soon everyone would know about it. It was appalling for me to stand by and witness what was going on.'

'I can imagine it was,' said Carole. 'And, at the time of Anita Garner's disappearance . . .?'

'Yes?' There was a note of resignation in the woman's voice.

'. . . you and Harry had an alibi. You were on a trip to France on *Harry's Dream*.'

'Yes.'

'Was that true?'

'No. But,' she asserted, 'nobody questioned it. As I said, nobody at Footscrow House knew about the affair back then, so Harry wasn't a suspect or anything. And the police very quickly lost interest in Anita's disappearance.'

'What do you think happened to her?' asked Carole, quite harshly.

'I don't know.' Veronica Lasalle spoke as if that was the only answer she would offer, whatever the provocation. Whether she did know or not, it was hard for Carole to judge.

But she had a go at getting more detail. 'You hoped people would believe that your husband had killed himself?'

'Yes.'

'For that to be credible, he must have had a reason. Guilt for having killed the girl?'

'No. Fear of all the gossip starting up again would have been sufficient.'

'Hm. So if he wasn't with you on *Harry's Dream* on the way to France, where was Harry that Tuesday?'

'Like an ordinary day off. Round the house. Doing ordinary stuff.'

'You didn't live in at Footscrow House?'

'No. Thank God. We seemed to spend every waking hour there.'

'Did Harry ever stay there overnight?'

'Very occasionally. If there was a major crisis, one or other of us might stay there.'

'Did Harry stay there that Tuesday?'

'I told you. He was round the house. At home.'

As with her previous answer about what had happened to Anita Garner, Veronica Lasalle wasn't going to shift an inch from that position.

'All right,' said Carole. 'Coming up to date, how did you kill your husband?'

'It wasn't too difficult. I'd followed through every stage of the building – or rebuilding – of *Harry's Dream*. I knew as much about that boat as he did. And on a couple of previous occasions, we'd had problems with the heater, carbon monoxide leaking. So, sabotaging it wasn't that difficult.'

'Presumably, you did that while it was on the hardstanding at Fethering Yacht Club?'

'Yes. I was still a member there, so I had my own key-card. The Saturday evening, I waited until the barman had locked up and gone home. Then I let myself in, sabotaged the heater and left another bottle of whisky there, to be sure. Harry had told me he was going out fishing early on the Sunday morning, but I knew he would do more drinking than fishing. He had another bottle with him. I knew what I'd done wouldn't be guaranteed to kill him. If it hadn't, I'd have had to try something else.

'As it turned out, though,' she concluded with a smile of satisfaction, 'my first attempt did the business.'

There was a long silence. Then Carole asked, 'So, what are you going to do now?'

'I'll hand myself in to the police.'

'Oh?'

'I thought I could get away with everyone believing that Harry had topped himself. But clearly I can't. You aren't the only person round Fethering who's convinced it was murder. It's only a matter of time before the police come to question me. So, I thought I might save them a bit of trouble by confessing. That means they won't have to go through all kinds of elaborate investigations.' A wry, defeated smile. 'Very public-spirited of me, isn't it?'

'You have thought through the consequences of confessing, haven't you?'

'Oh yes. And I don't reckon they're too bad. I haven't got many years left. The idea of spending them in prison won't really make a lot of difference. Not having to think about cooking for myself, that'll be a bonus. And, really, there's nothing left in my life. No Harry now, and Roly's very rarely in Fethering these days.

'It means Harry's reputation won't be ruined. I will have saved him from having to go through all the police investigations and the trial and what-have-you.'

Veronica hadn't noticed the slip she had made, but Carole picked up on it. The widow had virtually admitted that she thought her husband had killed Anita Garner.

'Really,' said Veronica Lasalle serenely, 'it was a mercy killing.'

SEVENTEEN

Carole Seddon felt quite smug. She had completed the investigation on her own. She knew who had killed Harry Lasalle and, very satisfactorily, the perpetrator was going to confess to the police.

Carole felt pretty sure that she now knew what had happened to Anita Garner. Veronica Lasalle had effectively admitted that her husband had killed the girl. Whether she knew what he had done with the body was a question that no doubt the police would be raising with her during intensive grilling.

Part of Carole wanted to ring Jude on her mobile, just to crow about what she'd achieved. But she curbed the instinct. If Jude was going to swan off without telling her friend where she was going, then she would have to wait for news of Carole's triumph.

It was a good feeling to have such an explosive secret to impart, thought Carole. And impart it she would. In her own good time.

Meanwhile, in a drab front room in Liverpool, the very-much-alive Anita Garner – or Mary White – was still talking to Jude, who had just explained how she had heard the name Pablo from Shona Nuttall.

'Shona. She was a nosy cow. Always snooping on me and Pablo.'

'But were the two of you having affair?'

'Certainly not.' She was shocked by the idea. 'We may have been falling in love, but we weren't having an affair. We were both good Catholics.'

'But did you get the passport because you were going to visit him in Spain?'

'Yes. That was the idea. I don't know whether it would ever have happened. Pablo's mother was ill. The plan was that I would go out to Cádiz to meet his family and then, if they approved of me . . . I don't know. That was the plan. It didn't happen.'

'So, did you ever meet Pablo again?' A small shake of the

head. 'Or were you in touch with him again?' The same reaction. 'But did you tell your parents about your plans?'

'No.'

'Did they know you had applied for a passport?'

'My mother knew I had applied for it, but she didn't know why. I never told her. My father didn't even know I'd made the application. My father was . . . I had to find the right moment to tell him and it never came. He would have been appalled by the idea of my following a boy out to Spain. He had strict rules about relationships.'

'But you say yours with Pablo was perfectly innocent.'

'My father would never have believed that.'

'Hm.' Ideas were beginning to take shape in Jude's mind, explanations for the events of thirty years before. But she didn't yet have enough data to firm them up. 'Your Catholicism is very important to you?'

'It is the most important thing in my life. I draw great comfort from the Catholic Church. It dictates everything I do, every decision I have ever made.'

'And you're attached to a church up here?'

'Of course. The Metropolitan Cathedral. People still call it "the modern one", though it's been around since the Sixties. Known locally as "Paddy's Wigwam". I'm very involved with the community there. Do a lot of voluntary stuff.' A pale grin. 'Though, of course, ironically, I live this side of town in the shadows of the Anglican Cathedral.'

Jude got a feeling that the fullness of this answer was a stalling tactic, a way of postponing the more personal questions that must inevitably follow.

'You know, Mary, that I'm here because of Glen Porter.'

'Yes.'

'Where does he fit into your story?'

'Well . . . We were at school together.'

'I heard that.'

'But we didn't know each other very well.'

'He said he took you out a couple of times.'

'Yes, but he only wanted sex and he wasn't going to get any of that, so it didn't last.'

'Then why is he apparently the only person in Fethering –

possibly the only person in the world – who knows what happened to you?'

'Ah. We met again later.'

'When he was at university up here?'

'Yes. We just met on the street one day. I was in a bad way.' She coloured at the recollection. 'A very bad way. I was actually begging. Glen saw me and recognized me. He took me for a hot meal and he . . . transformed my life.'

'Oh?'

'I don't know if you've heard but Glen unexpectedly came into a lot of money?' Jude nodded. 'And he had plans to set up various charities abroad, but he said to me . . . that charity begins at home.'

'So, he helped you?'

'Yes. More than just helped. As I say, he transformed my life.'

'How?'

'He bought me this flat, for a start.'

'Very generous.'

'Yes. And he made me an allowance, to see me through, until I could get back into full-time working. And he rings to check that I'm OK, every month or so. If I've got a financial problem . . . you know, like I need a new freezer or something . . . Glen pays for it.'

'And does he . . .' Jude didn't know how to put this tactfully – 'does he expect anything in return?'

Mary White looked puzzled for a moment, then realized what the question meant. 'You mean, do Glen and I have a relation-ship? Am I his mistress?'

'Yes, that was more or less what I was asking.'

'No.' The woman again looked shocked. 'It's nothing like that. I wouldn't get involved in that kind of set-up. Glen Porter is just a very generous, charitable man. I've never had a relationship with anyone.'

This last sentence was spoken with a kind of perverse pride. And suddenly Jude had an image of Mary White as a woman above the lusts of the flesh, a kind of secular nun. It was not a path that she would have chosen for herself, but she could respect those who had that kind of vocation.

'What we haven't established yet,' she said, 'is what actually happened in Fethering, what made you cut yourself off from your family and come up here.'

'No, we haven't.' And the woman's tone suggested she thought that to be a satisfactory state of affairs.

But Jude had to find out more. She used her intuition, piecing together details from things Mary White had said. 'It's something to do with that room, isn't it? The room where the handbag was found?'

'Maybe.'

'Were you staying there that night, the night it happened?'

Mary White nodded uncomfortably. They were encroaching on events she had no wish to remember.

'Were you raped, Mary?' asked Jude.

Tears welled in the woman's eyes, then there was another, almost imperceptible nod.

'And that was why you left Fethering? You couldn't face your father after what had happened to you?'

'No, I couldn't.' A silence. Then, with mounting intensity, the thoughts and emotions which had been dammed up for so long were allowed to flow. 'I felt so dirty. I felt disgusting. It was my fault. I shouldn't have let myself get caught that way. I screamed but that didn't stop him. I shouldn't have stayed that night. I should have known I was putting myself at risk. It was my fault,' she repeated.

'It wasn't your fault,' said Jude gently, 'but I can understand how you must have felt.'

'All I could think was that I had to get away. I couldn't face my father, not after what I had allowed to happen to me. It would have destroyed his life.'

'You were in shock.'

'I don't know. Maybe. All I knew was that I had to get away. I rushed out of the room . . .'

'Leaving your handbag behind.'

'I wasn't in a state to worry about handbags. It was early in the morning, early on the Wednesday morning. I just ran away to Fethering Station. I caught the first train up to London, and then on up to Liverpool. I wasn't really aware of what I was doing. I just needed to get away.'

'And didn't you think of contacting your parents? You must

have known what a state they would be in. Surely, once you'd calmed down a bit, you could have given them a call?'

'Yes. I intended to. But, by the time I had made the decision to call them, something else had happened.'

Intuitively, Jude knew. 'You found out you were pregnant?'

A small nod acknowledged the truth of this. 'How did you know that?'

'I suspected it when you said Glen subsidized you until you could "get back to full-time working". And when you said you couldn't contact your parents, that confirmed it.'

'Right.'

'So presumably you had the baby?'

'Of course,' she replied sharply. 'I'm a Catholic. I couldn't *not* have the baby.'

'No. Of course not. Boy or girl?'

'Boy. Francis.' She nodded to the picture of the saint on the wall. 'After him.'

'So, you gave birth on your own?'

'In a hospital run by nuns. They weren't very forgiving to unmarried mothers back then. Light on the pain relief. "You got yourself into this situation, you have to suffer for it", that was their attitude. But it was worth all the pain, all the problems, all the difficulties. I got Francis.'

'So, he must be . . . what? Round thirty now?'

'Twenty-nine.' She couldn't keep the pride out of her voice.

'And does he live here with you?'

'He did, till a couple of years ago.'

'So, where is he now?'

'Francis tried a lot of jobs but none of them was a fit for him. He got very low, not being able to find the right way in his life. Then, finally, he did what he always should have done, what I always, in my heart of hearts, knew he would do.'

'And what was that?'

'He's at the seminary. Oscott College down in Birmingham. He's going to be a Catholic priest.' The pride in her voice redoubled as she said this.

'Congratulations,' said Jude. It somehow seemed appropriate. 'But . . .' Again, she had to get the wording right. 'You haven't told me who Francis's father was.'

'No. And I'm afraid that's the way things are going to stay.'

'If it was Glen Porter . . .' Jude fished, 'that would explain why he supported you financially. A guilty conscience . . .? A feeling of responsibility . . .?'

'It's my secret, Jude. Allow me that.'

'Yes. I would normally . . . but . . .' She had another go. 'If it was Harry Lasalle, then it might explain his death, either as—'

'I'm not going to tell you, Jude.'

'No. No. Well, fair enough. I'm grateful for all you have told me.'

'I only did tell you stuff because Glen asked me to.'

'I know. And it must have been hard for you. Thank you.'

'Right.' Suddenly businesslike, Mary White looked at her watch. 'I have to go down to the cathedral. There are some preparations I help with before the seven o'clock Mass.'

'Yes, of course. Thank you so much for your time and for . . . all you've told me. Rest assured, I won't do anything that's going to disrupt the life you have up here.'

'You'd better not,' said Mary White grimly.

As she was led through the hall, Jude noticed a framed photo-graph on the wall. It looked like a studio shot, head and shoulders, of a man in his twenties. 'Is that . . .?'

'Yes, that's Francis,' said the proud mother.

And, suddenly, as Jude noted the hair colour and the unusual teeth, everything fell into place.

EIGHTEEN

As Sunday turned into Monday, Carole's frustration mounted. She didn't stay permanently behind the curtains of her sitting room waiting for her neighbour to return, but she did peer through them quite often. When she passed by, taking Gulliver for his Sunday afternoon walk, there was no sign of life from Woodside Cottage. Nor was there the following morning when woman and dog once again set off for Fethering Beach. Nor when they came back.

Carole's desperation to reveal to her collaborator how she'd solved both cases grew more intense. But there was no way she would give in and ring Jude's mobile. She had her pride. She never wanted to sound needy.

And she understood the basic principle that revelations are all the more effective when delayed. It was annoying, though.

It was too late when Jude got back from Liverpool to get from Euston to Victoria to catch the last Fethering train from Victoria. So, she rang a former lover who had a flat in Covent Garden and asked if he could give her a bed for the night.

He could. And, in fact, generously he let her share his. Old habits died hard, so, for old times' sake . . . Very pleasant it was too.

And it distracted her a little from the challenge which the Monday held for her.

She left Covent Garden early and was on a Fethering-bound train by eight o'clock.

Footscrow House. She had to make a start at Footscrow House. She remembered Pete the decorator saying he'd be working back there after he'd finished her sitting room. And, sure enough, she recognized his van parked in front of the building.

The front door was open and there were fewer building workers and decorators around than there had been on the day of the handbag's discovery. She heard movement from upstairs and went up to find Pete once again working in the room, one end of which had been the staff bedroom when Footscrow House was a care home. He was sanding down the window frames, preparing them for repainting.

He turned at the sound of Jude entering the room. Toothy grin once again. 'You haven't come to complain, have you? Not happy with the job I done at Woodside Cottage?'

'No. Very happy with that, Pete. Not so happy with other things.'

'Oh?'

'Were you sailing at the weekend?'

'No, bit too nippy for me. Went into the yacht club Saturday lunchtime for a drink, like I usually do.'

'Yes. Much talk about old Harry Lasalle, was there?'

'Not a lot. Only the old members really knew him, and there's been a whole lot of new people come in. Blokes who're doing more "working from home". Adjusting their "work/life balance", that's what they keep talking about. Seem to have more time for sailing, anyway.'

'Lucky them.'

'Yeah.'

Jude looked round the opened-out room. 'Pete, can you think back to when you were decorating here, when Harry Lasalle was winding down the care home business?'

'Oh, right. Time of Anita Garner's disappearance – back to that, are we?'

'If you don't mind . . .?'

'No skin off my nose.'

'And that bit, over by the alcove, that was a separate bedroom? The staff bedroom?'

'Yes. We've been through this before, haven't we, Jude?'

'We have, but there are still details I'm trying to work out. I've now heard a suggestion that Anita Garner slept in that staff bedroom the night before she disappeared.'

'I wouldn't know about that,' said Pete. 'Weekend, wasn't it? I wouldn't have been here.'

'It wasn't the weekend. It was a Tuesday.'

'Oh?'

'Do you know if Harry Lasalle was here then?'

'No idea.' He sounded defensive now. 'Could have been, I guess. He was the boss. He owned the place.'

'Who else might have been around?'

'I don't know. Residents, visitors, nursing staff . . . Usual people you'd get in a care home.'

'Hm. I just wondered—?'

But, before she could ask her next question, Jude was interrupted.

'You!' said a voice from the doorway. 'I thought I'd told you to stop meddling.'

Roland Lasalle. A very angry-looking Roland Lasalle, short and bustling. He turned to Pete. 'And you, you lazy bugger! Chatting her up again when you should be working.'

'Listen, Roland, I—'

'Shut up! Get out! I need to talk to this bloody mischief-maker.' Cowed, Pete made for the door. 'And shut it behind you!'

Jude and Roland Lasalle looked at each other, each assessing their options.

He spoke first. 'So, I dare say you feel very pleased with yourself.'

'Why should I?'

'Well, you've solved the mystery, haven't you?'

She had, of course, but how could he know that? Unless he'd been in touch with the woman who had been Anita Garner in Liverpool.

'I don't know what you're talking about.'

'My mother went to Fedborough Police Station yesterday evening and confessed to having killed my father.'

'Oh?' Jude looked blank.

'Don't pretend you don't know! It was your bloody next-door neighbour spreading rumours in the Crown and Anchor that made her realize the game was up.'

This was news to Jude. Clearly, Carole had been conducting her own investigation, but it was no time to be distracted by the details of that. 'Roland,' she went on, 'this space must be very familiar to you.'

'What do you mean? Of course I know Footscrow House. I got involved in a lot of my father's doomed projects here. And now that I'm in sole charge, I'm going to be involved in one that will actually work, will actually make some money. No more Fiasco House. Footscrow House's holiday flatlets are going to be a little gold mine for me. Not so little, actually.'

'I wasn't talking about the building as a whole. I was talking about this specific room.'

'Oh?'

'Or, more particularly, that bit of the room over there. Where there used to be a wall which was one side of the care home staff bedroom.'

'What are you talking about?'

'I'm talking, Roland, about a night, some thirty years ago, when you broke into that room and raped Anita Garner.'

'That's ridiculous!'

'No, it isn't. It's what happened. And, after Anita ran out of the room, you noticed she'd left her handbag. So you prised the covering of that alcove open and hid the handbag there. Where it stayed until a couple of weeks ago.'

'You have no proof of any of this.'

'Oh no? Would you believe that yesterday I was talking to Anita Garner?'

'No, I wouldn't. And, if she's still alive – which I very much doubt – she'd never testify against me.' Jude was rather afraid that might be true. 'Not, of course, that I did anything wrong. Rape? Do I look like a rapist? Why would I have to resort to rape when I can get any woman I want?'

Jude wasn't about to argue over the rationale of the rapist. She knew it rarely had much to do with sex. It was all about power.

'And your parents covered up for you, didn't they, Roland? Or rather, your mother did. She always protected you. Couldn't let anything nasty happen to her precious Roly, however badly he behaved. But she didn't mind suspicion building up against her husband – in fact, she probably encouraged it – so long as no one questioned the integrity of her Mummy's Boy.'

'Stop it! This is all nonsense!' Roland Lasalle was definitely losing his cool.

And Jude was having difficulty controlling her anger. To her mind, rape was one of the most despicable of crimes. And when she thought of the consequences of Roland's actions on the life of Anita Garner, her fury knew no bounds.

'I bet your mother's protecting you again right now. The whole Anita Garner story was being resurrected – that was unfortunate, wasn't it? If the police got involved, they could soon prove that your father had nothing to do with the girl's disappearance. But that might lead them to start questioning you.'

'They'd have no reason to.'

'No? And, once the police started questioning you about Anita Garner, they might also get interested in how your father died.'

'What on earth has that to do with anything? The police already have a solution to the crime. They've heard my mother's confession.'

'But suppose your mother didn't do it? Suppose you actually—?'

'Oh, for heaven's sake! I'm not going to listen to any more of this slanderous nonsense! I'll have you know what you're saying is actionable, and I command the services of some of the best – and most expensive – lawyers in the country.'

'Oh yes,' said Jude gleefully. 'Do let's bring in the lawyers. Then the police will really have to investigate more rigorously.'

'Let them investigate!' said Roland recklessly. 'They'll be wasting their time. There is no proof that I ever did anything wrong.'

'Oh, but there is.'

'What do you mean?'

'Not on your father's murder, perhaps . . . though I'm sure detailed police work could find some. But on the rape of Anita Garner, there's very definite proof.'

'I don't believe you.'

'Have you heard of DNA testing?'

'Of course I have.'

'Well, Roland, you have left your mark in an indelible way. When you raped Anita Garner, you got her pregnant. Yes, you didn't know you had a son, did you?' It was Francis's red hair and prominent underbite, the physical likeness he bore to his father, plain to see in the photograph in Mary White's flat, that had explained things for Jude.

'You're lying!'

'No, I'm not. Your son is in a seminary in Birmingham, training to be a Catholic priest. So, he's another inconvenience, but not one you can get out of your life very easily. And your mother can't do it either.'

'I could kill him,' said Roland Lasalle with icy precision. 'It wouldn't be the first time.'

Jude saw it all. 'You killed Harry, didn't you? You killed your father. Your mother knew what you'd done. So, she once again tried to protect you by confessing to the murder.'

'She did it,' said Roland coldly. 'She knew what had happened between me and Anita.'

'The rape?'

'It wouldn't have been rape if the bloody girl had cooperated. I was only after a bit of fun. But then she resisted and that made me mad. Just as it would have made any other red-blooded man mad. So, I had to teach Anita Garner a lesson. It was her own bloody fault!'

'Her own fault, just for being a woman?'

'No. Oh, you wouldn't understand.'

'Wouldn't I?' asked Jude. 'Your father found out what you'd done, didn't he?'

'It was only because the bloody girl screamed. He heard her when he was doing his rounds that night. He was on his way up to investigate when the girl rushed past him on the stairs. He chased after to try and stop her. I saw the handbag and hid it, so nobody would know Anita had been there.

'I met my mother on the landing. She worked out what had happened. If there was ever any investigation, she said we should put the blame on my father.'

'But why?'

'Because I had my whole future ahead of me and he was just a washed-up has-been. Anyway, there never was any investigation, not into my having sex with the girl.'

'You raping the girl, you mean,' said Jude implacably.

Roland Lasalle shrugged. 'Whatever.'

'But there was intensive investigation into her disappearance, wasn't there?'

'So I heard. I was spending most of my time in London by then. I wasn't involved.'

'But your father was. He had to put up with all the rumours . . . about him having had an affair with Anita Garner, about him having murdered her. He was the one who suffered.'

'It blew over,' said Roland dismissively.

'It took a long time to blow over.'

'But it was the right thing to do. Mummy worked it out. She said that allegations like that could have ruined my career. It was better that people suspected Daddy than me.' He spoke like a petulant child.

'But didn't you feel any guilt?'

'Guilt? Why should I feel guilt? Because some girl made a fuss about me wanting to have sex with her?'

Jude looked at Roland Lasalle in disbelief. How could anyone be so obtuse, so unaware of the consequences of his actions? Though maybe, if someone had been brought up by a besotted mother, who let him do anything he wanted, who told him everything he did was right . . . Yes, it figured.

She spoke, guided by intuition but knowing she was right. 'You thought it was all over, didn't you? But then, the accidental discovery of the handbag you'd hidden and probably forgotten about . . . that brought all the rumours back to life again. And put the pressure back on your father. And this time he wasn't so keen to help you out, to protect you, was he?'

'You'd aced him out of this development project, hadn't you? The conversion of Footscrow House to holiday flatlets. You didn't want Lasalle Build and Design involved here, did you? And suddenly your father thought, "Then why should I play ball? Why should I relive all those allegations about me and Anita Garner? If I'm questioned again, why don't I tell the police that my disloyal son was the one who raped the girl?"'

'So, when he actually told you what he'd decided, you knew you had to keep him quiet.' There was a silence. 'Am I right, Roland?'

'If you were right,' he responded coolly, 'you'd have a hell of a job proving it.'

'I've told you. The proof exists . . . currently living in a seminary in Birmingham.'

Various emotions were reflected in Roland Lasalle's face. Then fury took over. 'So, what if I did kill my father?' he demanded, bullying. 'How do you feel, being alone in a room with a murderer? Safe? Huh?'

He leapt at her, his hands suddenly constricting the soft flesh of her neck, his body clamped to hers in a parody of an embrace.

There was not enough air in her lungs for a scream but – thank God – some sound must have escaped through her gasping mouth. Thank God, because Pete, waiting on the landing, rushed back into the room and, with a couple of sharp punches, flattened Roland Lasalle to the floor.

He hadn't been a very good criminal. Once the police started investigating Veronica Lasalle's confession, they found all kinds of anomalies. And her account of having let herself into Fethering Yacht Club to sabotage *Harry's Dream* was quickly disproved by a check on the footage of the CCTV cameras that covered the hardstanding in front of the club.

While the recording showed no sign of Veronica Lasalle, it did of course show her son entering the yacht club and setting up the carbon monoxide booby trap on the boat. Not a very good criminal. His boarding-up of Anita Garner's handbag thirty years earlier hadn't been a masterstroke either.

Roland Lasalle was duly charged with the murder of his father.

His other crime, the rape of Anita Garner, never came to court. Though evidence of his guilt existed, in the form of Francis White, the incident was not relevant to the police's murder enquiries. Anita Garner's disappearance remained unexplained, though still occasionally pontificated upon by Barney Poulton in the Crown and Anchor. He still supported the view that Anita Garner's remains would in time be found in a shallow grave on the South Downs. As he would explain at great length to anyone who came into the bar.

The lack of investigation into the rape was welcomed by Mary White in Liverpool. Her life continued as she wanted it to, busy with her charitable work for the cathedral and looking forward to the day when she would see her precious son, Francis, ordained as a Catholic priest.

NINETEEN

'Well,' said Carole tetchily, 'I would have thought getting a confession of murder is a very good outcome for any criminal investigation.'

'Oh, I agree,' said Jude, suppressing a smile, 'but of course there are lots of reasons why people confess to crimes. And it's not always because they committed them.'

That got a characteristic Carole Seddon 'Huh'.

'Incidentally,' said Jude, 'I had a call from Brandie yesterday.'

'Oh yes?' Carole feigned complete lack of interest.

'You know she went off to the weekend course in Homeopathy in Wales . . .?'

'No.' Carole did know but she wasn't going to pretend that the doings of Brandie Neville held any interest for her.

'Apparently, she got totally caught up in Homeopathy. She thinks it's the most wonderful therapy ever invented.'

'Which one is it?' asked Carole, who again knew full well. 'Is it the one where you drip candlewax on to stones on people's backs?'

'No,' said Jude patiently. 'It's the one where you treat people with a substance which has been diluted many times.'

'Why?'

'Because its practitioners believe that it will effect a cure.'

'So, let me get this right, Jude. You take a medicine and you dilute it many times, in the hope that the dilution will make it more effective . . .?'

'More or less, yes.'

'. . . whereas logic and common sense would dictate that, the more a medicine is diluted, the less effective it will become.'

'You might think so, yes.'

'I do think so. And do you believe that Homeopathy works, Jude?'

'In fact, I don't. I think it's a pseudoscience which is completely ineffective.'

'Oh, that's very comforting.'

'What's very comforting?'

'The fact that there are certain areas of mumbo-jumbo you don't believe in.'

'Thank you, Carole,' said Jude, inured to such gibes. 'Anyway, Brandie has decided she wants to be a Homeopath.'

'Does she? Well, I suppose there's no law against it. But what does this mean, in terms of Brandie's *personal development*?' She loaded the last two words with mock-seriousness.

'It means that Brandie no longer wants to be a healer.'

'Oh? So that rather lets you off the hook.'

'Yes.' Jude was not too upset by Brandie's news. The more time she spent with the girl, the less she had trusted her tenacity. Yes, Brandie had been madly keen on healing for a while. But Jude had expected that soon to be replaced by another enthusiasm for another fad. Which is exactly what had happened.

'So, is she going Homeopathize in Fedborough?'

'No. Brandie's moving.'

'Oh.'

'It seems that her new relish for Homeopathy has been matched by a new man on the course who shares her enthusiasm for the therapy. In Wales.'

'Ah. I always thought she was a very shallow person.'

'I think . . . it hurts me to say this, Carole, but I think you're right,' said Jude, fully aware of the enormous satisfaction her neighbour would get from her words.

Carole smiled serenely. 'So where will this . . . change of circumstances . . . leave Ted?'

'In the lurch, I'm afraid,' said Jude. 'Which may in fact be a rather better place for him.'

'Yes, yes. I think you could be right,' said Carole with something like smugness. Of course, there was no longer anything between her and Ted Crisp, but there was no denying that she had seen off the odious . . . and very shallow . . . Brandie Neville.

There was a part of Jude's conversation with Ted in the Crown and Anchor which she hadn't reported to her neighbour. The landlord was more relaxed talking about certain subjects to Jude than he would have been to Carole. After he had maundered on for a while about how bereft he felt without Brandie, Jude was sufficiently emboldened to say, 'And dare I ask what the sex was like? Did that work?'

'I don't know.'

'I'm sorry?'

'Well, thing is, Brandie was keen on doing this tantric sex.'

'Ah.'

'It seemed to take forever. I'm afraid I fell asleep.'

'Ah,' said Jude.

But the influence of Brandie Neville was not completely obliterated. On the Crown and Anchor menu there remained the 'Vegan Option', the 'Shepherdless Pie'.

Barney Poulton developed quite a little routine about 'meat-free alternatives', with which he would bore anyone in the bar who hadn't made their escape quick enough.

The knock-on effects of Fred Givens's 'working from home' destroyed the marriage. He and Lauren divorced. Her hopes that she would then move in cosily with Glen Porter were quickly dashed. He broke off the relationship and started to spend even more time abroad. There, he attended to his various forms of philanthropy, while in Fethering his image as a selfish playboy remained unchallenged.

And he continued to stay in touch with Mary White in Liverpool. And apply his charity there when she needed it.

Francis White duly became the Catholic priest his mother had always wanted him to be.

And Mary White, whose experience of men was restricted to one brutal encounter, continued to draw great comfort from her faith.

After a time, Fred and Lauren Givens drifted back together and, to the general surprise of Fethering, remarried. The village consensus was that they must have found a way of making it work, though probably, in their second marriage, without spending so much time together.

And the supply of ceramic toadstools to the gift shops of the South Coast continued uninterrupted (definitely without marketing advice from Fred Givens). The Tinkling Red Polka Dot turned out to be the bestseller.

After the news of Roland Lasalle's arrest had been all over the media, Carole rang Malk Penberthy and suggested meeting for a coffee in Starbucks. When they sat down with their coffees, he was almost pathetically grateful.

'I'm so glad you got in touch, Carole. I was rather afraid you might not.'

'Why wouldn't I?'

'I don't know. I just wondered, now you know the identity of Harry Lasalle's murderer, whether you'd want to continue listening to the circuitous maunderings of an elderly gentleman.'

'You mustn't think like that, Malk. It's always a great pleasure to see you.'

'Oh yes. The pleasure is reciprocal.' Suddenly fearful, he asked, 'I'm not sounding pathetic, am I? I don't want to give the impression that I'm lonely.'

'No, no, you don't sound like that at all.' Carole could identify with the fear. She had felt it herself. To her – as, it seemed, to Malk Penberthy – the worst thing in the world was to let people think you were lonely. 'You're still very interested in everything. I'm sure you lead a very full life.'

'Yes. Yes,' said the old journalist, almost as if he were trying to convince himself. 'Of course, I have my birding.'

'Of course. And your work at Fedborough Wetlands Centre.'

'Yes. Though that's getting a bit difficult with the eyesight.'

'Oh?'

'Macular degeneration.'

'I'm sorry.'

'Yes. Not the greatest qualification for someone going bird-watching – the inability to see any birds.'

'No. Not great.'

'Also makes reading difficult. And reading always was a great resource for me. Still . . .' He dwindled to silence.

Carole couldn't think of anything very helpful to say, but Malk Penberthy revived and continued, 'I'm glad that the mystery of Harry Lasalle's death has been solved . . .'

'Yes.'

'. . . though it's a pity we never found out whether there was a link between that and Anita Garner's disappearance.'

Though it was said as a statement, Carole knew that he was really questioning her. And she felt terrible as a result. She and Jude had talked about the situation at length, and both agreed that they should keep quiet about what had happened to the missing girl. Any lapse of security might threaten Mary White with exposure and bring on her the cruel burden of publicity which she had managed to avoid for so many years. And possibly even revive the trauma of her rape.

'Yes,' Carole agreed uncomfortably with Malk, 'it's a pity.'

He grinned at her. 'And might I be correct in the assumption that you do know rather more about that aspect of the case than you are vouchsafing to me?'

'You are correct,' replied Carole wretchedly.

'My respect for your integrity dictates to me that you have a good reason for keeping such findings secret. A matter of confidentiality, I surmise . . .?'

Carole nodded.

'Which being the case,' he said in his customary orotund manner, 'I will not press you for further information. I am fully apprised, from the system of ethics I followed during my journalistic career, of the necessity of protecting one's sources.'

'The situation is analogous to that,' admitted Carole, finding that she was slipping into Malk's speech mannerisms.

'I would like, if I may, Carole, to ask you one question. You are fully at liberty to answer it or not to answer it, according to your conscience, but it is something I have longed to know for many years. It is a question which I believe you to be in a position to answer, should you wish to do so. I will, of course, leave it to your finely tuned judgement.'

'Very well, Malk. What is your question?'

'Is Anita Garner still alive?'

Carole thought for no more than a nanosecond. What possible harm could it cause to answer the question? Had Malk Penberthy still been a thrusting young journalist, avid to get a scoop for the *Fethering Observer*, the situation might have been different.

But she had the same respect for his integrity as he had for hers.

'Yes,' she said. 'She is still alive.'

His expression of relief, the way the tension drained out of his thin body, showed how much the revelation meant to him, how long he had been bottling up anxiety about the missing woman.

'Thank you, Carole,' he said. 'That is all I wanted to know.'

It was early in the summer that Carole heard the news of Malk Penberthy's death. She was one of very few who attended his funeral at Clincham Crematorium. To her surprise, she found out from the Order of Service that he had been ninety-seven years old. She would miss their conversations in Starbucks.

Cheated of spending her declining years in prison, Veronica Lasalle spent them visiting her son in prison. She maintained the view that her husband's death had been suicide and that her beloved Roly's incarceration was a cruel miscarriage of justice.

Roland Lasalle's property development company did not survive its boss's conviction. The conversion of Footscrow House into holiday flatlets was suspended. Another property developer bought the building cheap, with the intention of opening it as an arts centre (the surest way of losing money next to owning racehorses).

It looked as though the name 'Fiasco House' would continue to be justified for some time to come.

And Pete? He continued to go from decorating job to decorating job, never having to resort to advertising to get work. His knowledge of – and collection of – eighteenth-century glass grew, and he longed for retirement when he could devote more time to his hobby. But every time he mentioned the 'r' word to his clients, they became very distressed and said there was no one else who could do their decorating for them. Certainly no one else who would be so amenable to 'Oh, while you're here . . .', 'Could you just . . .?' and 'Would it be possible for you to . . .?' requests.

He kept up his membership of Fethering Yacht Club and won many more trophies there.

Pleased with her new-look sitting room, Jude asked Pete, the decorator about whom no one in Fethering ever had a bad word, to paint her bedroom. They spent some time discussing colours. Carole said they could do a lot worse than magnolia.